"I'll do right by them," he vowed. "No matter what."

"While I may have only just learned of the twins' existence, I'm going to be a big part of their lives." It sounded like a warning. "I can tell you right now that being the kind of dad who visits every other weekend isn't going to be enough for me. We'll have to learn to work together. It isn't going to be easy."

She'd been the one who'd turned down his proposal, who had broken his heart. It didn't matter why. Not to him. If only things had been different, maybe then she would have said yes when he'd gotten down on one knee. But that wasn't what had happened, and she had to deal with life as it now was.

"I'm sorry," she said, knowing it wasn't nearly enough.

"For what?"

Where did she even start apologizing for all that had happened?

The silence between them was deafening. At long last, she spoke.

"For everything."

A *Publishers Weekly* bestselling and award-winning author of over forty novels, **Deb Kastner** enjoys writing contemporary inspirational Western stories set in small communities. Deb lives in beautiful Colorado with her husband, miscreant mutts and curious kitties. She is blessed with three adult daughters and two grandchildren. Her favorite hobby is spoiling her grandchildren, but she also enjoys reading, watching movies, listening to music, singing in the church choir and exploring the Rocky Mountains on horseback.

Bonding with the Babies

DEB KASTNER

LOVE INSPIRED
INSPIRATIONAL ROMANCE

LOVE INSPIRED®

INSPIRATIONAL ROMANCE

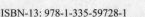

Recycling programs
for this product may
not exist in your area.

ISBN-13: 978-1-335-59728-1

Bonding with the Babies

Copyright © 2024 by Debra Kastner

For questions and comments about the quality of this book, please contact us
at CustomerService@Harlequin.com.

® is a trademark of Harlequin Enterprises ULC.

Love Inspired
22 Adelaide St. West, 41st Floor
Toronto, Ontario M5H 4E3, Canada
www.LoveInspired.com

Printed in Lithuania

MIX
Paper | Supporting
responsible forestry
FSC® C021394

And Ruth said, Intreat me not to leave thee,
or to return from following after thee: for whither
thou goest, I will go; and where thou lodgest,
I will lodge: thy people shall be my people,
and thy God my God.
—*Ruth* 1:16

To my forever love, Joe.

Chapter One

Whoever it was who first said *go big or go home* had obviously never had to go home miserably humiliated with a broken heart and his tail tucked between his legs.

Frost Winslow had.

Over a year had passed since that awful day, but he still remembered—and felt every painful moment—as if it were yesterday.

But life had gone on, even when he'd felt as if it might not. One day at a time, one step at a time, he kept living his life. Whenever he felt alone and abandoned, he'd remind himself of the blessings of being surrounded by a large, supportive family. He couldn't ask for anything better than his brother and four sisters to pull him up when he was falling.

This evening found him where he was every Friday night—performing at open mic night at Sally's Pizza. He strummed the chords on his guitar without conscious thought, absentmindedly singing and filling the notes of the folk song with a depth and emotion he wasn't experiencing. He didn't feel much of anything anymore. His heart was an empty, gaping hole, but he still managed to fake it enough to be able to perform in front of small audiences made up of local townspeople and family he knew well. That's what it meant to be an entertainer, he would remind himself—to put on a brave face even when he wasn't really into it, which was most of the time nowadays. But his guitar was one of the few things that gave him respite and peace, so he kept showing up on Friday nights. Kept playing and singing.

His mind once again drifted back to the day he'd had the brilliant idea to propose to his girlfriend, Zoey Lane, in front of her entire college symphony orchestra. He'd planned everything to perfection, from working out the surprise with the conductor to sneaking into the practice to taking over and making the huge announcement.

It had been an enormous mistake, and one he deeply regretted with every pore of his being.

How was he supposed to know she would refuse him when he'd gone down on one knee, leaving him red-faced and stranded with a diamond ring in his hand?

They'd been in love back then. He'd been so certain she'd say yes. There was no reason for them not to become engaged—at least he thought so at the time.

But she hadn't said yes. And she'd avoided returning to their small mountain hometown of Whispering Pines, Colorado, since that day, too—thankfully. He'd often thought of how it would be if he ran into her again, which would no doubt happen at some point, though he hoped it wouldn't be soon. A year wasn't long enough.

Frost finished his folk song and glanced up, smiling at his captive audience, all of whom were enjoying their dinners at one of the few places to take a date or spend time with the family on a Friday evening without leaving town. Rather than speaking between songs, he smiled, nodded his thanks, and launched into a familiar hymn.

The bell over the door rang and his heart jolted to life as he watched Zoey enter the restaurant. She looked up and their gazes locked.

She was here!

The song dropped from his lips as he swallowed hard, his mouth suddenly dry. He couldn't believe his own eyes as she moved toward the stage area with her mother beside her. Zoey's caramel brown hair was longer than it had been the last time he'd seen her, and her face paler, but it was her, all right. He felt her presence with every fiber of his being. Even after all this time, it was as if they were compellingly drawn to each other. They'd always had a special connection, a magnetic pull from one heart to another.

To his surprise, he realized that bond hadn't changed. Not after all the time apart nor after everything they'd been through together.

What *had* changed, he realized as he stopped strumming his guitar mid-tune and Zoey approached the staging area with a determined set to her jaw, was that she wasn't alone. On her hip, she carried a baby with a mop of curly blond hair wearing a blue onesie. In the other arm she carried an infant carrier with a second baby who was sound asleep with a pink-and-purple crocheted blanket tucked around her and a big yellow bow on her head.

"Zoey," he said aloud into the microphone, his tone cracking under the sudden pressure. Realizing his voice was echoing throughout the restaurant, he quickly turned off the mic, cleared his throat, and set his guitar aside on its stand before hopping off the stage and approaching the woman he'd once loved with his whole heart.

His mind spun with question after question.

When had she gotten pregnant—and had a baby?

No.

Not one baby.

Two.

Twins.

He hadn't thought his heart could break any more than it already had, but seeing Zoey again, especially with babies in tow, completely shattered him.

"Zoey," he repeated, scrubbing his hand through his hair as he gave the baby boy on her hip a closer look. Her mother moved to Zoey's side and took the car seat with the baby girl to a nearby empty table. "What are you doing here?" he asked.

It was a stupid question. She had as much right to be here as he did. Whispering Pines was her hometown, just as it was his. She'd been born here and had grown up here. But it had been so long since she'd been back—since well before the day she'd turned down his proposal.

Why had she chosen now to return?

"Can we go somewhere quiet where we can talk?" Her voice was little more than a whisper as she adjusted a white knit scarf across her neck and tucked her hair behind her ears. "I'll leave the babies with my mom for now."

He glanced around the restaurant. It was unusually quiet at the moment, and more than a few gazes were on them. He could have heard a pin drop as people stared at them in open curiosity. Other than his five siblings, most people didn't know the story behind the botched proposal, because he hadn't been about to share his humiliation with the world. But in as small a town as Whispering Pines was, the fact that Frost and Zoey had once been a couple and obviously now weren't wouldn't have passed by unnoticed.

"I... I... Sure," he stammered, gesturing toward the door. "Just let me get my jacket." While Zoey passed the baby boy to her mother, he jogged back up to the stage and grabbed his wool-lined jean jacket and tan cowboy hat from the back of the chair where he'd hung them earlier, keeping his head down and desperately trying not to meet anyone's gaze. He considered announcing that he would finish his set when he returned. But he honestly didn't know when or if that would be, or what emotional shape he'd be in after he spoke to Zoey, so instead he waved to Sally, who gave him a brisk nod of understanding in return. She would take care of any announcements that needed to be made.

He held the door for Zoey and ushered her out before him, unconsciously brushing the small of her back until he realized what he was doing and dropped his arm as if his fingers had been singed by fire. The blast of cold winter air and swirling snow that hit him as he stepped out the door matched his frozen heart, and he inwardly cringed.

"Are you...did you have anywhere specific in mind that you wanted to go? We can take my pickup if you'd like," he suggested.

She shuddered and ran her hands over her arms, which were covered by a teal-blue down puffer jacket. "Yeah, okay. It's too cold out here to walk. The heater will be welcome."

Frost nodded, then gestured her toward the back of Sally's restaurant where he'd parked his truck earlier in the evening. He unlocked the pickup with his key fob and opened the passenger door, reaching for her hand to help her climb onto the high seat. She glanced at his palm and ignored it, choosing to scramble into the vehicle on her own.

He hesitated after he slid behind the wheel, tossed his cowboy hat on the back seat, and put his key in the ignition, turning on the truck so it could warm up. A flurry of emotions rolled over him like the snowstorm outside—anger mixed with heartache and confusion.

But mostly he was furious.

He squeezed the wheel with both fists and glanced at her.

"Where to?" he asked, his voice gravelly.

"Um," she said, then hesitated, dropping her gaze from his with a sigh. "It doesn't really matter, Frost. Just somewhere we can be alone to talk. The park, maybe?"

"Yeah, okay." He pulled the truck around and drove to the park without saying a word, his head still spinning with questions, though he voiced none of them. Instead, he gritted his teeth. What could she possibly have to say to him now that she hadn't said a year ago when he proposed to her?

When they reached the parking lot nearest the playground, he pulled into a space but left the engine running to keep the warmth flowing, not that he could feel it.

He continued to squeeze his fists on the steering wheel, breathing through icy lungs and staring straight ahead as he waited for her to speak.

"I'm sorry it took me so long," she whispered, her breath misting despite the heater blowing warm air.

"For what?" he snapped.

"Seriously, Frost? Are you going to make me say it?"

He turned his head to meet her gaze, hardening his

features. He didn't want her to see how much her words pained him. He shook his head. "Say what?"

"I know I've waited far too long for this, but I've finally come home because of the babies."

"What?" he asked, confused, even as the angst of understanding washed over him, instantly drowning him.

"Your—" she started, but her voice cracked, and she had to try again. "*Your* babies. Didn't you see the twins in there? They both look just like you."

"My…*babies*?" He tried to take a breath but couldn't. His lungs weren't working, and his heart surely wasn't.

Was she telling him that those babies were his biological children? How old were they? He was doing mental calculations in his mind, but the truth was he didn't need to.

He wanted to deny it, and he opened his mouth to do just that, but no words emerged, because denying reality was pointless. In the end, he could only find one question worth asking.

"How?" His voice was still gruff and had dropped a good octave lower than usual.

"Frost!" she exclaimed, raising her palms to her flushed cheeks.

"No, I'm sorry. That's—that's not what I meant. But… considering the circumstances, I just don't get why you would…"

She broke her gaze away and turned to look out the passenger window. "They're your babies. You can take a paternity test if you want, but all you really need to do is look at them to know for sure. Dante and Ariella both have your blond curly hair, your blue eyes and that Winslow cleft in their chins."

"Zoey," he said gently, but she didn't respond. "Zoey," he said with more force, reaching for her jaw to turn her face toward him. "I believe you."

And he did.

The world had tilted on its axis and there wasn't enough gravity on earth to hold him to the ground, but he did believe her words.

He was no longer a single man with no strings attached.

He was no longer a man who could chase his own dreams without thinking of how they would affect others. All his plans for the future were gone in a flash.

He was a *father*.

Of twins.

Zoey thought the worst part was going to be telling Frost he was the father of their twins. As it turned out, that was merely the beginning of the barrage of questions, and with each query came an additional stab of pain so sharp she wasn't sure how she could endure it.

And yet she did. Because she had to. It was only right.

"Did you know you were pregnant when I asked you to marry me? Is that why you turned me down?"

"What? No! I didn't…" She trailed off into silence, not willing or able to offer the explanation he was so clearly expecting. "I found out I was pregnant a few weeks after your proposal."

"Why did you wait so long to come to me with this? You should have reached out the moment you found out you were pregnant," he accused brusquely. "I can't believe you hid them from me."

"I wasn't hiding them," she protested, but she couldn't say more.

"These babies are as much mine as they are yours. I've missed so much of their lives. I would have been there for you from the beginning. I'd have been there for our children."

If Zoey had been absolutely certain the babies were Frost's when she'd first learned she was pregnant, she probably—no, she *would* have reached out to him before the babies were born and would have given him the rights he was now demanding. But she'd had so much more to deal with at the time that she hadn't been able to think about anything else. She'd been wrestling with a great deal of emotional and spiritual distress that had nothing to do with Frost and everything to do with her pregnancy.

If the twins hadn't been Frost's...

She couldn't even go there. Not after all she'd suffered.

The truth was far more traumatic than anything Frost could dream up, even if he tried. Because the reality was, she *hadn't* known for sure that Dante and Ari were Frost's children until about two months after they were born, when their hair had started growing in curly blond and the color of their eyes had solidified into Frost's beautiful shade of silver blue.

And even then, it had taken her months to get up the nerve to bring them home to meet their father. Every day she waited made it that much harder to face Frost with the truth—or at least what she was able to admit of it.

"I decided it would be better for me to face my life as a single mother rather than have someone else involved." That was only part of the truth, and not the worst part, but it was all she could say right now.

"Wow." Frost slammed his palm against the steering wheel and stared out the driver's side window. They sat in silence for a long, painful moment. "I'm not *someone else*, Zoey. I'm their *father*."

"I'm not trying to hurt you," she said raggedly. "You know I would never do that."

"No?" His voice rose in pitch. "Because that's exactly what you're doing. How could you… I thought we were…" he stammered, then swallowed hard. "I was going to put a ring on your finger. I *proposed* to you, Zoey. I loved you so much. I thought we were solid, that we'd marry and have a family and grow old together. I would have protected you and the children, even if everything was done in the wrong order. I would have stayed by your side. We could have faced it together. Man, this is messed up in so many ways."

"Yes, it is," she agreed. If only she could share with him just how *messed up* her life had become. But she couldn't. Not now, and probably not ever. A migraine was coming on and the moonlight created a painful aura she tried to blink away to no avail. Her ears were ringing incessantly.

"So, what now?" he asked in a gravelly tone. His tenor voice was usually so rich and smooth. She knew how much it was costing him to have this conversation with her.

"Well, now that you know the twins are your children, I suppose that's your call." The ice pick pounding on her temple was getting worse by the minute, and she could hardly put two thoughts together. Her neck was so tight with strain she could barely turn her head, so instead she shifted her whole body so she could look at him.

"My call. *My* call?" he said, resentment dripping from each syllable. "Well, thank you very much for finally including me, Zoey. Hitting me with this news out of nowhere after all your months of pregnancy. And however old the twins are now. Congratulations, Frost. You're a father."

Her heart ached. This man was her sweet, gentle, soft-spoken Frost, a sensitive man who cared for everyone he met and who had a special place in his heart for animals of all kinds. His strained reaction showed her just how badly she'd hurt him with all the decisions she'd made. But it was too late to take it all back, and she wouldn't even if she could. She'd thought long and hard about this decision, before returning to Whispering Pines.

As difficult as this was, Frost deserved to know about the twins.

She wasn't the only one who'd been wounded, but for her it was because of what had happened to her that awful night in her dorm room, which to this day she couldn't quite remember clearly, but that had sent her whole life into a tailspin. The damaging chain of destruction continued to grow with every breath.

"What I meant was, you have choices in what you want to do in regard to the twins," she clarified. "I'm not expecting anything from you. Not time. Not attention. Not money."

He scoffed and shook his head. "After all this time, how could you even say that? You really don't know me at all, do you?"

Of course, she did. That's why she hadn't reached out back when she'd first discovered she was pregnant and hadn't been positive whose children they were, and why she'd only now returned home.

Because she'd known exactly how he would react. Maybe not the initial shock or the anger that followed, though she didn't blame him for that. Anyone would feel the same.

She hadn't been sure what to expect reaction-wise when she told him the truth. It had been impossible to guess how he'd respond to suddenly discovering he had children. But she knew beyond a doubt he wasn't the type of man who would walk away from his babies or forego what he considered his responsibility to them in every way.

She was trying to let him know she shouldered all the responsibility. He needn't step in just because she'd suddenly reappeared in his life.

A low, pained sound escaped his throat as he shoved his fingers through his hair. "I want—*need*—to get to know my babies. What did you say their names were? Dante and Ariella?"

"Yes. Dante and Ariella, but I call her Ari for short."

"Dante and Ari," he repeated, his rich tenor curling gently around the words, softly cradling them with his voice. "My children."

"I'm sorry this has come as such a shock to you. I thought about calling you first, but I felt this was something we needed to address face-to-face and not over the phone."

That she'd chosen a public place to first approach him had been a premeditated decision because she was too much of a coward to bring the twins to him in private. She now recognized that had been spineless on her part and unfair to Frost. Now the whole town knew about Frost and the babies. Word would spread quickly to those who weren't frequenting Sally's tonight. But what was done was done. Better to dive into the deep end than wade into the shallow end.

"How do you want to go about this?" he asked. "I'd like to meet my babies and get to know them, find out all I missed out on. And the sooner, the better."

"You can come by my mom's house tomorrow if you want. That's where I'm staying until I can find a place of my own."

"You're staying in Whispering Pines permanently?"

Did she hear a hint of hope in his tone? It gutted her. But they had to be mature about this. Co-parenting wasn't going to be easy on either of them no matter what choices they made. "Honestly? I don't know right now. It depends on how certain things work out for me."

"For *you*? If you don't stay around, it's going to be much harder to co-parent," he pointed out with a dark scowl, making her sound selfish for even considering living anywhere besides Whispering Pines.

"I know. We have a lot to talk about, and we both have many decisions to make where the kids are concerned."

He made a low, guttural sound in response.

"Here's the thing. I have an audition for the Colorado Symphony Orchestra coming up in about a month's time. My future plans depend on whether or not I get in. If I do…" She let her sentence drop and hesitated a moment before picking it back up again. "I'll be around, at least in Colorado, though not necessarily in Whispering Pines. If I don't make it, my Plan B is to give Broadway a shot."

He finally turned to face her and lifted an eyebrow in surprise. "Broadway? New York City?" His voice had raised an octave, but then he shook his head and took a deep breath. "Of course you'll get into the symphony. No question. You've been practicing nonstop on that violin of yours since you first picked it up in elementary school. I hardly remember a time when you weren't toting it around."

"You know, back when I was a kid, I hated my mom for making me practice so much. It started out with an hour a day and grew as I did. Every second was painful. I hated playing and I didn't understand why she forced the issue."

"And yet you were first chair all through high school—and college, too, if I'm not mistaken."

"I know, right? After all my grumbling and complaining when I was younger, it's now my violin that may take me places I could only imagine and give me the life for which I now dream. But for all the work I've done, it doesn't necessarily mean I'll pass my audition into a professional organization. There are so many excellent musicians out there coming in from all around the world."

"That may be, but I have no doubt you'll be accepted." He sounded much more confident than she felt.

"And yet even after all the hours I spent in practice, I'll never be half the musician you are. I learned music through extensive, excruciating hours of practice, while you…" She shook her head and let her sentence hang.

"Hmm." It was neither an agreement nor a denial. Frost was a natural musician, having taught himself both guitar and piano without the use of written music. That had come much later, when he'd first considered studying music in college. His voice was a smooth, rich, honeyed tenor that vocal lessons couldn't impart. But he'd never advanced with his skills, never done anything beyond open mic night at Sally's Pizza and the bonfires the Winslows often held at their farm for family or guests. Zoey had always privately wished they could have gone to college together as they'd planned. But it hadn't worked out for Frost. He had to stay and work the family business at that time.

"So—about the twins. Tomorrow?" she asked, bringing the conversation back to him visiting with the babies.

"That's a definite yes. What time do you want me?"

"How about ten o'clock?"

"Sure. Okay." Once again, he scrubbed a hand through his already messy hair, something Zoey knew was his individual tell that showed just how anxious he was feeling. It was a habit she recognized from when they'd dated in high school. She knew him so well. It was sad where they'd both ended up.

"It'll be all right," she assured him. She started to reach out to touch his arm, but when his gaze dropped to her hand, she quickly withdrew it. "You'll be great with the twins. You've always wanted to be a father," she reminded him.

His frown deepened and he shook his head with a hard jerk. "Not this way, Zoey."

"No," she agreed. "Not this way."

"I'll do right by them," he vowed, his jaw tightening around the words. "No matter what."

"I know you will."

"But Zoey?"

"Yeah?"

"I want you to know right now that while I may have only just learned of the twins' existence, I'm going to be a big part of their lives." It sounded like a warning. Frost's silver-blue eyes were glinting with ice.

"I would expect no less from you. And I know there's a lot to work out between us where the children are concerned. But I also don't want you to feel as if I'm forcing you into doing anything that you don't want to do."

"You know me better than that. Dante and Ari are every bit as much my children as they are yours."

"Yes. Of course." She wondered what she'd just agreed to. He was right, though.

"You wouldn't walk away from them, and neither will I. One of the first things we need to do is make plans on how to co-parent, how to share time between the two of us. I don't have any idea how these things are done, but I can tell you right now that being the kind of dad who visits every other weekend isn't going to be enough for me. We'll have to learn to work together. It isn't going to be easy."

The migraine that had been brewing in Zoey's skull zapped her like a stroke of lightning.

Or maybe it was his words.

She'd been the one who'd turned down his proposal, who had broken his heart. It didn't matter why. Not to him. That was entirely on her, as was any resentment he now held against her for her actions.

If only things had been different. If only that horrible night at the dorm hadn't happened. Maybe then she would have said yes when he'd gotten down on one knee. They could have married, albeit quickly, and they could have done things mostly in the right order.

But that wasn't what had happened, and she had to deal with life as it now was.

"I'm sorry," she said, knowing it wasn't nearly enough but needing to express the feelings in her heart anyway.

"For what?" Once again, his fists clenched the steering wheel so hard his knuckles whitened.

She folded her arms tightly around herself and shuddered, feeling suddenly cold despite the heat flowing through the cab.

How did she even start apologizing for all that had happened?

The silence between them was deafening. At long last, she spoke.

"For everything."

Chapter Two

Frost arrived at Zoey's mom's house with ten minutes to spare. He'd taken care of all his morning chores caring for the farm's many animals much earlier in the morning. Along with the draft horses they used to pull the sleigh in the winter and the hay cart in the summer, they had a half dozen riding horses and a petting zoo, including donkeys, llamas, goats, sheep and more. Even the chicken coop was Frost's domain.

He hadn't slept a wink last night. The weight of his new circumstances made it next to impossible to breathe as he pictured his twins—his *babies*—and thought about every-thing they entailed. He had enough nieces and nephews to know infants required tons of paraphernalia and even more time and attention.

Zoey was right about one thing—he'd always wanted to be a father, especially after he'd grown up and watched all five of his siblings marry the loves of their lives and go on to become parents. He wanted that for himself. It was perhaps the deepest desire of his heart, the one for which he prayed the most. He'd once even believed that dream life would be with Zoey, and he'd thought she wanted the same thing with him. So why had she taken so long to admit she'd become pregnant after that one special night they'd spent together? He should have waited, and he knew it, but the twins—he felt with his whole heart that babies were always blessings. Hadn't Zoey known that about him?

But after she'd turned down his very public proposal... well, he'd never thought fatherhood would happen, at least not this way—having children before he was happily married. Worse, he couldn't imagine co-parenting with the woman who'd shattered his heart.

How was this going to work, if they couldn't even stand to be in the same room together? He could barely think of Zoey's beautiful face without his gut churning as if a backhoe was digging around in his belly. He was still so angry, and fury like that wasn't going to go away quickly. Now he'd have to see her all the time, spend time with her and interact with her, because he wasn't going to let his children grow up being passed from mother to father and back like a football. They were going to know their daddy was there for them, not occasionally, but all the time. Anytime they needed him.

But even as he thought about it, he realized how much fatherhood scared him. The sum total he knew about being a dad was being the *fun uncle* to his nephews and nieces. That wasn't a lot to go on. At least he'd held a baby before and wasn't afraid of curling a newborn infant in his arms. And the twins weren't even newborns. At four months they would be holding up their heads and working on strengthening their muscles. More than that, he knew how to change a diaper and feed a baby a bottle, so he wasn't starting at ground zero. But he wasn't sure how he'd feel when it was his own children he was cuddling and caring for.

Would it be different?

For some reason, it felt like it would be. As their daddy, every single thing would seem more overwhelming.

Taking a deep breath, he climbed the steps of Zoey's mom's porch and paused with his finger hovering just over the doorbell. There were babies in the house and ringing the doorbell might startle them.

He decided to knock instead.

Zoey answered the door immediately, their baby girl in her arms, wide-eyed and clinging to her shoulder—almost as if she'd been waiting for him on the other side.

"Here you go," Zoey said, immediately placing Ari in his arms as Frost entered the house. "Meet your daughter, Ari."

Ariella. His *daughter*.

Frost swallowed hard and curled his arm around her, peering down at her soft features and wide, silver-blue eyes that mirrored his. "Hello, sweet thing," he whispered, his voice ragged with emotion. "Nice to meet you. I'm your daddy."

Ari reached for Frost's free hand, clenching his thumb in her tiny fist and bringing it to her mouth, gumming it noisily.

Frost chuckled. "Is she teething?" he guessed as he cheerfully wiped the drool from her chin with the cloth Zoey handed him.

Zoey laughed along with him. "She's been miserable with it. Those bottom two teeth are about to cut and she's chewing on everything."

"She's a strong one, isn't she?"

"Just wait until you hold Dante. He's a real bruiser. He came out two pounds heavier than his sister."

"Who was first?" he asked, shifting Ari up toward his

shoulder. There were so many things he didn't know—about her pregnancy, everything that had happened at the babies' birth, and the four months following. Ari was teething, and it made him think about all the milestones he'd already missed.

"Ari was first. At least she'll be able to hold that fact over Dante for the rest of his life, no matter how big he gets."

"Ba-ba-ba-ba," Ari agreed, kicking her feet enthusiastically.

"Already talking, is she?" Frost asked, touching her nose with the tip of his finger. "How about *da-da*?"

"She's definitely starting to babble. She's quite talkative. Sometimes in the evenings she'll talk herself to sleep. She hasn't said da-da yet, but I'm sure that's coming soon," Zoey agreed. "Especially as you spend some time with her. I've been coaxing her on *ma-ma*, but from what I've read, that consonant will come along later."

"Speaking of moms, where's yours today?" he asked, wanting to say hi to Lizzie, the woman who'd practically been a second mother to him while he and Zoey had been dating. He'd seen her around at church but hadn't spoken to her since the big breakup. He didn't know how much Zoey had told Lizzie about his proposal, and he'd been too embarrassed to ask.

"She went out shopping with friends in Denver. I think she wanted to give us some privacy this first time with the kids."

Frost caught Zoey's gaze and her smile wavered. This was a lot for Frost to handle all at once, and he could tell Zoey felt the same way.

"I don't want to rush her," he said, kissing Ari's chubby

cheek. "I'd rather savor each moment as it comes. I'm glad I'll be there when she starts saying *da-da*." He tamped down the anger that jolted through him at having already missed so many *firsts*. "What about Dante? Is he talking yet?"

"Not a whole lot. He makes gurgling noises and howls a lot louder than Ari when he wants something, but he hasn't put any consonant-vowel combinations together yet."

As if Dante knew they were talking about him, Frost heard a loud, voracious, *pay-attention-to-me* howl coming from the baby monitor sitting on the dining room table.

"Speaking of Dante," Zoey said with a laugh. "I imagine you'd like to spend some time with your son, as well."

"Of course," Frost agreed. "While you're getting him up, I can change Ari's diaper. Just point me toward the changing table."

Zoey's gaze widened in surprise. "You're actually offering to change her? I mean, you can if you really want to, but you don't have to."

"Don't look so shocked. My brother and all my sisters are married now, so I have a bunch of nieces and nephews to spoil. I'm totally comfortable with babies, even newborns. I've done my fair share of babysitting and diaper changing since…" He let the sentence drop, mostly because he felt as if he'd been sucker punched and didn't have the air left to finish speaking. The ache in his heart was more painful than he'd ever imagined it could be, not even when she'd turned down his proposal. Now, interacting with his children—it was almost too much for him. He was floored by the physical sensations he was experiencing.

Zoey chuckled, but it wasn't a happy sound, more like

she was trying to breathe through a strangled throat. "I can just picture you as the fun uncle. You're the one who takes the kids to the park, builds forts out of blankets, and reads them stories in the dark with a flashlight, aren't you?"

"And I change diapers," he reminded her. "More than that, I actually enjoy it, because babies are so happy and interactive when I'm getting them fresh and clean. Point me in the right direction for diaper duty and go get our son before he screams himself hoarse."

"What do you say, little miss?" he asked as he gently laid Ari on the changing table in the corner of the living room. "Let's get you dry and comfortable."

He was telling the truth when he'd told Zoey he really didn't mind diaper changes. He'd found it to be a great time to interact with babies—when they were bright and alert. Despite the circumstances that had brought him here, knowing this beautiful little baby was his daughter filled him with a sense of joy he hadn't imagined possible. She was so precious with her soft blond curls and her big blue eyes blinking curiously back at him.

Zoey returned with Dante, a stocky baby who significantly outweighed his sister. He had the same curly blond hair and large blue eyes as his sister, but his cheeks were fuller, the cleft in his chin was deeper and his arms and legs were a great deal chunkier than Ari's were. Still, Frost could tell they were twins—and they were most definitely his children.

No question there.

"Wanna trade?" Zoey asked, holding Dante out to Frost.

They exchanged infants and Frost changed Dante's diaper as well, with Zoey observing over his shoulder. A shiver ran up Frost's spine at her nearness. He could hear her breathing, feel the warmth between them, and he swallowed hard. Even after all this time, she didn't so much as have to touch him to cause him to respond to her presence.

"I'm impressed," she said, pressing her palm to the back of his shoulder. "You're right. You are an expert. I'll never doubt you again."

"Hmm," he agreed. It was all he could manage.

He might consider himself an expert at some things about babies—changing diapers being one of them.

But knowing he was a father to these two precious children and all that entailed?

Not even close.

Zoey sat cross-legged on the couch with Dante, who was curled in her arms and noisily slurping from his bottle. She had to hold the bottle tightly because Dante liked to bat it with his fists, and more than once he'd sent his bottle flying when Zoey wasn't paying enough attention to him. Staying completely focused on the babies was something she'd learned early on in motherhood.

She didn't know what she'd expected when Frost had come over to spend time with the babies, but this wasn't it. She certainly hadn't expected him to be such an expert with his children. Silently, she watched him sitting in the rocking chair with Ari tucked close to his chest, curled in his strong arms as he fed her a bottle and sang to her in the lovely, rich voice Zoey remembered so well. It made her heart clench in a way she never could have imagined when she'd decided to return to Whispering Pines to make things right between them.

She'd thought she was prepared, or at least as prepared as she could be.

But she'd been wrong.

She now realized things might never be right between them, and that broke her heart. It wasn't that she expected he'd ever want a relationship with her—or maybe deep down, she *had* hoped things could change.

But of course, that wasn't possible.

She'd known it was going to be hard to see Frost again and to introduce him to their babies. She'd known without a doubt he would step up and want to be a father to the twins. That was just the kind of man Frost was. He felt the same way toward Dante and Ari as she did. Babies were a blessing no matter how they were conceived.

What she hadn't expected was that her attraction to him hadn't lessened, not even after all this time and everything that had happened between them. It hadn't occurred to her that her convoluted feelings would still be involved.

And now, seeing him with their twins in his arms?

It was just too precious, and almost more than she could bear. Her throat burned with emotions she'd never before experienced, and she tried hard but to no avail to swallow them away. It was a different kind of feeling, watching a man become a father. As the twins' mother, she was the only other person who knew the power of that love.

When she'd first returned, she hadn't thought much beyond introducing him to his children, mostly because she'd told herself the next move was his—even though she already knew what that move would be. And although he'd immediately made it clear he wanted to play a big part in their lives, she was unsure how that would work out in practice.

Frost lived here in Whispering Pines, working for the family business just as he'd done since he was a youth.

She doubted he'd give that up even if he could. When push came to shove and the Christmas tree farm went through a bad year, he'd prioritized his work over college to get it back on track. The Winslows were a close-knit family, and she knew Frost found great joy working with the many animals and ferrying those who visited the Christmas tree farm on a sleigh or a hayrack.

And though she'd come home for now, she had dreams that would take her back to Denver, which was an hour-and-a-half away from the small town. A commute, if not unworkable, was at least not comfortable, especially if she had to leave the twins behind when she was busy playing or practicing with the symphony. The more time she was forced to be apart from them, the worse it was going to be for her.

She could always get an apartment in Denver. It wouldn't be impossible to co-parent from that distance, but she could already tell that Frost wouldn't like being separated from his babies any more than she would, which was understandable. Still, how did people work co-parenting out in practice? Did one parent have to give up their dreams in order to be near the other? Or did one parent have to concede not to be as much in his or her children's lives as they would prefer?

Frost adjusted a pink-and-white-striped burping towel onto his broad shoulder and expertly shifted Ari, gently patting her back to get the bubbles out as he finished his song and kissed her chubby cheek.

"I'm going to have to learn more lullabies," he whispered.

His quiet country song was definitely working, lulling Ari into a sound sleep. Meanwhile, Zoey shifted Dante to her shoulder, and he promptly let out a big, juicy belch, smiling up at her and looking pleased with himself.

Frost chuckled. "That's my boy."

His eyes locked with hers. She knew him well enough to be able to read the anger and betrayal written on his features as he realized just what he'd said, that Dante was his child. She couldn't blame him for that.

"She's knocked out. Do you have cribs set up for them?" he asked as he stood, slowly rocking back and forth to keep Ari asleep.

"I've got a couple of Pack 'n Plays in the guest bedroom where I'm staying," she answered. "Ari's is the yellow one, and Dante's is green."

"All right. Let me put this precious girl down for a nap. Then we can talk."

Zoey's stomach turned over at the change in Frost's tone—there was now a tightness to it that had taken over from the sweet lilt he'd been using earlier with Ari. She had a feeling she wasn't going to get the same gentle treatment as their daughter had. Rather, she was in for an interrogation for which she wasn't prepared.

Since Dante had just taken a nap, he was wide awake, so she placed him on the floor on a play gym with toys arching over him and lullaby music gently playing from a speaker that he could kick with his feet. He stuck his fist into his mouth and sucked loudly. Unlike Ari, he wasn't particularly interested in working on expanding his vocabulary, nor did he pay much attention to the mirror that reflected his face back to him. He preferred to play with his toes and bat at the fluffy lamb hanging just over his head.

Zoey returned to the couch and sighed, pulling her legs in to her chest, wrapping her arms around them and hugging them tight. As Frost entered the living room, she turned her focus inward, to her breathing.

"So," Frost started without preamble. "Are you going to tell me why you didn't contact me as soon as you knew you were pregnant, or do I have to guess?"

It was the first question she'd expected him to ask, but try as she might, she couldn't find the courage to answer it truthfully. Instead, she simply said, "No."

He frowned. "No? You aren't going to tell me? That's all you have to say to me? Are you serious right now?"

She broke her gaze from his and shrugged.

"So let me get this straight. You didn't think I deserved to know I was going to be a father? Despite the fact that half their genetic makeup is mine."

"It's not as simple as all that."

"I think it is," he said through gritted teeth.

Humiliation and shame washed through her, and she had to stifle the sobs rising from deep within. How could she tell him she hadn't known if the babies were his until well after they were born? Maybe he'd understand if she explained the circumstances…

No. It was too soon to visit that dark part of her life, even for Frost. She couldn't talk about it yet.

"Please, Frost. Don't press me. I promise I will tell you everything and explain to your total satisfaction. But not now. I just can't do this today."

"Zoey?"

She looked up and he caught her gaze, taking her measure. She felt as if he was reaching deep into her soul, and she wondered if he could see the blackness there.

"I don't know what's going on, but I'm not going to pressure you," he said softly after a long, tense moment of silence. "With that said, there's still a lot more we need to talk about. I'm anxious to spend time with Dante and Ari as soon as possible. And my family will be eager to meet them, as well."

"Of course," she said, cringing inwardly when she thought of the number of people in his family she would soon be encountering. Five siblings and their spouses… and they'd all be judging her for keeping Frost's babies a secret from him, wouldn't they? If their places were switched, she certainly wouldn't think very highly of what she'd done to their brother and would probably carry animosity for the betrayal. If it wasn't enough that the twins were a huge surprise, she'd broken Frost's heart when he'd proposed to her. She couldn't expect to be easily forgiven for that.

"Will you be attending church with your mom tomorrow morning? We could maybe meet up then."

She paused a moment and then shook her head. She wasn't ready to face the whole community, not now that they knew she'd returned a single mother of twins.

And that was nothing to say of facing God, in church or even in her own heart.

She and the Lord weren't currently on speaking terms, and she hadn't been to church since that horrible night in the dorms. She privately acknowledged that it had been her own stupid decision to attend that party. But wasn't God supposed to be watching over her even when she made mistakes?

Where had He been then?

Frost appeared surprised that she was clearly hesitant to attend church. Back when they were dating, she'd been new to Christianity and Frost had been encouraging her along the path of faith. At the time she'd had great interest in attending church with Frost, but not so much now. Anyway, she wasn't keen on trying to reconcile with his family in such a public place.

"How about you come over to the farm tomorrow evening to visit?" he suggested, scrubbing his fingers through his hair. Her gaze turned to his messy curls and her breath caught. He'd become even more handsome, if that were possible. He'd matured a lot over the past couple of years. His facial features were more masculine and defined. He'd lost the baby face that made the girls chase him in high school and had covered his dimples with a light beard. That, and he wasn't smiling. "I'll set up a bonfire, and whoever in my family can make it can come meet the twins. You haven't met everyone yet, and I'm sure they'll put aside whatever plans they have to spend time with Dante and Ari."

Zoey nodded but couldn't voice an answer.

"Invite your mom, too," he suggested. "It's been a long time since she's attended one of our famous bonfires. Oh—and maybe bring your violin? We can play a few duets like we used to?"

Zoey tried to swallow but couldn't. The Winslow family bonfires were some of her very favorite memories ever, and she carried them close to her heart. Roasting marshmallows for s'mores, the happy glow of everyone's faces against the radiance of the crackling fire, smiling and laughing at the buzz of upbeat conversation, Frost playing his guitar, and her accompanying him on her violin. Well, she would be fiddling, technically, which was especially fun for her since she usually played classical music. The whole family would join together in song, and with the

Winslows' amazing vocal harmonies, it often sounded as if there were more voices even than people surrounding the firepit. Like a beautiful choir. Sometimes there would even be a country dance or two, or Frost's brother Sharpe would do tricks with his dog.

Still, a bonfire seemed like as good an idea as any for everyone to meet the twins. All the adults would be in a good mood and would welcome the babies into the Winslow clan and pass them from arm to arm—even if they rejected her outright.

Which reminded her…

"I gave the babies my own last name on their birth certificates," she admitted, and Frost winced as if he was in pain. She couldn't explain why she'd chosen to go that route without getting into everything else she could not yet find the strength to explain, so she plunged ahead with what she *could* say. "I thought…if you want to, that is… we can have their last names legally changed to Winslow."

"Of course, I want that," he said, choking on his words. "No question that I want my children to bear my name. But you're okay with that?"

He had no idea just how *okay* she was with it. It was her first step in admitting to the world that the twins were Frost's babies. Hopefully the first step of many. She would have gladly named them Winslow from the start if she'd known for certain they were his.

Whatever else did or did not happen between them moving forward, she knew he would always be there for Dante and Ari, and that brought her a sense of peace she hadn't experienced in over a year. She wasn't alone in this. Not in parenting, anyway.

She closed her eyes and inhaled, but then pain stabbed

at her heart and her moment of peace was broken as she reminded herself that nothing had changed in her own life.

This was all about the babies.

As for her own turmoil? Well, she'd just have to push that aside.

Chapter Three

Frost hummed cheerfully under his breath as he hitched the two sleek, jet-black Shires to the sleigh. He hadn't been able to sleep again for most of the previous night, so he'd spent the time looking up famous classic lullabies and committing them to memory so he could sing them to his babies.

This morning, he'd spent time with his sister Avery and her husband, Jake, who had a whole passel of kids. He knew they'd be the perfect people to go to for advice on getting… *All. The. Things.* Because he had no clue about any of it. Two days ago, babies were the furthest thing from his mind, and now they were all he could think about.

It was truly amazing how his whole world had changed in an instant—and forever.

By the time his sister and brother-in-law were finished with him, he'd ordered for home delivery two infant car seats, a double stroller, two nifty swings that moved side-to-side as well as back and forth and that played lullabies, two cribs that he was going to set up in the room next to his that was currently serving as a guest bedroom, and a changing table. And that was nothing to say about the incidentals—diapers, wipes, a diaper bag, clothes of all sorts, toys, a play mat and dozens of other items Jake and

Avery insisted were necessary to take good care of babies. All the things would start showing up at the beginning of next week and would continue flowing in for probably a month or so.

Frost took a deep breath and swallowed hard, nuzzling his face into Jack's neck and scrubbing his fingers across Jack's chest under his muzzle, which was the horse's favorite spot for a scratch or two. He supposed his horses hadn't come with an instruction book, either, but he'd spent his entire life, for as long as he could remember, caring for the animals. He felt way more comfortable around them than he did around the twins—and they were his flesh and blood.

It had taken a good chunk of change out of Frost's savings to purchase everything the babies would need when staying at his house. He hadn't realized how much *stuff* would be involved. It was one of those things that he'd simply never noticed because he'd been a single man and baby necessities hadn't been a part of his life.

Now it was. But that wasn't even what was intimidating him so much. It wasn't the items themselves, but rather the thought of having to use all of them to help keep his babies happy and safe.

He checked the time on his cell phone. Zoey and the kids would be here soon.

Their children.

He wondered how long it would take for him to get used to those words and the gut-swirling feelings that always went along with them.

Zoey hadn't visited the farm in years, and a few things had changed since then. There was a popular petting zoo thanks to his sister Molly and her husband, Logan, and they now had more for visitors to do in the fall, including a fun pumpkin launcher created by his newest nephew—Sharpe and Emma's son Aidan.

Maybe the biggest change was that all five of his siblings had married and had children, either of their own or as the result of the marriages. The bonfires were much livelier with the little ones participating, at least until they curled up on their blankets or in their parents' arms and fell asleep to Frost's music.

He had such fond memories from when Zoey had been considered part of the family, when she'd bring out her violin and fiddle lively tunes as he accompanied her on the guitar around the snapping bonfire, and everyone would sing to the songs they knew. Those had been amazing times—nothing like he expected tonight to be.

There were bound to be some undercurrents of tension, as he and Zoey were tentatively working out the relationship between them. Still, tonight he was introducing his babies to his family. That part would be a real blessing.

"Are these two horses new?" Zoey asked from just behind Frost's right shoulder, causing him to jump in surprise and the drafts to shift restlessly because of his movement. The Shires Jack and Jill snorted, their nostrils flaring as they tossed their heads in alarm.

He murmured to the horses, settling them with gentle hands on their necks. His breath caught in his throat as he turned on the heels of his cowboy boots to face Zoey, who was carrying the twins in harnesses, Ari on the front and Dante on the back. "You just scared ten years off my life. You ought to be wearing a cowbell or something so people know when you're sneaking up on them," he teased. "And you," he said to the beagle stretched out next to his heel, "are the worst guard dog ever. You're supposed to bark in alarm when people sneak up behind me."

"I wasn't sneaking," Zoey informed him as she bent down to scratch the beagle's oversized, floppy ears. "Besides," she continued, her eyes shining, "I doubt that's going to be much of an issue for long. Not when I have the noisy twins with me. Between Ari's babbling and Dante's howling, you'll be able to hear us coming for miles. So, who is this guy?" she asked, gesturing toward the beagle. "Is he new to the program?"

"This guy," he answered, "is actually a girl. Her name is Daisy. My sisters rescued her for me. I'm training her to work in the court system as an emotional support dog."

"I don't know what that means."

"Daisy is useful when a victim—whether an adult or a child—must be a witness in court and face their abuser. Daisy's being trained to help calm the victim and help give him or her the support they need to get through a tough and emotional situation. It's like PTSD on steroids in that kind of situation."

"I've never heard of that before, but it sounds like a great use for an emotional support dog. I imagine that's got to be one of the most anxiety-causing situations ever." She shifted from one foot to the other, and for a moment, she broke eye contact with him and pinched her lips tightly together. He had the strangest feeling she wanted to tell him something.

But it was only for a few seconds, and then the moment passed, and she returned her gaze to his.

Frost ran a hand down Daisy's back. "It's amazing to watch and really is important to the people she helps. Daisy is excellent at what she does, especially when she's working with children. She helps calm them down and keeps them focused away from the bad stuff going on around them."

"Was this one of your sisters' ideas?" It was a reasonable question, since three of Frost's four sisters ran the service dog program at Winslow's Woodlands. "I know they've trained dogs in a variety of fields."

"It was my idea, actually," Frost said. "I first saw dogs being used in court on a television documentary. I couldn't get it out of my mind, so I asked my sisters to help me select Daisy from a local puppy mill rescue and to work out a training schedule for her. We're still rather new to it, but so far, she's doing great. She's a natural, as if she was born for it."

Zoey moved to the Shires, running her palm against the nearest one's muzzle. This time they didn't balk but rather leaned into her ministrations with a soft nicker. Frost knew how much Zoey had always loved horses, though she'd grown up in town and had never had a horse of her own. He'd often wondered if his accessibility to horses had been one of the things that had first attracted her to him. During high school she used to visit him at the farm, and he would saddle up a couple of the horses so they could go riding together.

"Didn't you used to use gray Percherons to pull the sleigh?" she asked. "Not that these two drafts aren't stunning."

"Meet Jack," Frost said, patting one Shire's neck. "And his partner, Jill. Our Percherons have been retired to the pasture to live their best senior lives." He paused for a moment, watching Zoey as she interacted with the horses. "Did you bring your violin?"

"I had my hands full with the twins and all their para-phernalia, so my mom is going to bring my violin with her when she comes for the bonfire later this evening. Come to think of it, though, I'd better text her to remind her to bring it."

Zoey pulled her phone from her front pocket and bounced on her toes to keep the babies sleeping as she texted her mom.

Her phone pinged and she gazed down at it, laughing.

"What's so funny?"

"My mom," Zoey explained, her lips twisting into a smile, "has just discovered emojis. Now she can't get enough of them."

She turned the screen so Frost could see the three full lines of smiley faces, multicolored hearts, puppies, kittens, and even a four-leaf clover.

What *wasn't* there was a clear answer to Zoey's text.

"Is that a *yes*, do you think?" Frost guessed. "With all the happy faces and everything?"

"Even the animal faces are smiley, so I suppose that's her way of saying she hasn't forgotten. Thank you for inviting her, by the way."

"Of course. She's always welcome." Frost nodded, but his smile felt pinched. When he and Zoey had been dating, her mother had often joined in the Winslow family bonfires, but she hadn't been to one since Frost and Zoey split up. It was one of those awkward family things Frost could never get used to, being close to someone and then suddenly not.

There was a lengthy, extended, and very uncomfortable pause between them as their gazes locked and held, before Dante broke the silence with a vibrant wail—not so much one of distress as outright anger. Clearly, he'd woken up wanting out of his sling.

"Do you have the *mads*?" Zoey asked her baby boy in a sweet, high tone. "Turn that frown upside down."

Frost was surprised at his own heart's reaction, immediately wanting to reach out and soothe the infant, to make everything better—as if he could. He hadn't carried the baby for nine months as Zoey had. He hadn't even known little Dante and Ari existed until a couple of days ago.

And yet...

Was this what it felt like to be a father? To respond at such a profound, basic level to his offspring calling?

"May I?" Frost asked, reaching for Dante, and wrapping his hands underneath the baby's shoulders, gently threading his legs out of the baby sling.

"Of course," Zoey said. "They're quite a load, carrying them both at the same time. I can't imagine how it will be once they've grown some. How am I going to be able to carry both of them at one time?"

Even one baby was a ton of work, much less two, and Frost silently vowed then and there to take some of the burden from Zoey, though he would never tell her so aloud. He knew how stubborn and independent she could be, and he didn't want her to shut him down before he could prove himself to be the man—the *father*—the children needed in their lives.

"I've got the sleigh ready to go, but I thought you and the twins might enjoy meeting some of our resident petting zoo farm animals before we leave for the bonfire."

Zoey's eyes lit up, just as he'd hoped they would. Dante and Ari might be a tad young to really appreciate the animals, but Frost hadn't forgotten that Zoey's favorite date had always been visiting a zoo, be it the Denver Zoo, Cheyenne Mountain in Colorado Springs, or even the Wild Animal Sanctuary.

"So, you may have noticed we have several barn cats hanging around now. I don't know whether you remember or not, but we didn't used to have kittens."

"Your sisters extended their rescue program to cats?" Zoey guessed with a chuckle. "Emotional support kitties?"

Frost snorted. "Hardly, although in truth there actually is such a thing as an emotional support cat. My sisters have enough on their hands keeping up with all the dogs they bring in. But yes, it is entirely my sisters' fault we have a new litter of cats running around. As usual, their kind hearts got the best of them, and they rescued a pregnant mama from sure destruction after being abandoned by the side of a highway. We were able to adopt out a couple of the kittens, but most ended up staying around here on the farm. Surprise, surprise," he said with cheerful irony in his tone.

"I'll admit I was wondering about that. I didn't remember you having any cats before." Zoey reached out to pet an orange tabby tiptoeing her way across a stall door, balancing with the natural grace of a feline, and looking at Zoey with interest.

"You know my sisters. They can't refuse any animal in need."

"Only your sisters? Not you?" He knew she was teasing him over his soft spot for animals of all kinds. His sisters weren't the only culprits. Taking care of the retinue of petting zoo animals and all the horses was his responsibility, and was much of the reason, other than money, that he hadn't attended college with Zoey. The timing just hadn't been right for him to leave the farm back then.

His heart suddenly felt weighed down.

"We have a llama," he said, trying to change the subject and lighten the mood. "He's getting his thick winter coat now and we'll have to shear him in the spring."

"I saw him on my way in. And who do we have here?" She moved to the stall at the end of the row and peered over the door, curiosity glowing in her eyes.

"These guys are Taco and Beans, our donkeys." Frost held Dante up so he could see the donkeys inside the stall. He didn't expect his young son to be interested in the donkeys, but Taco was evidently interested in the baby, and he nudged Dante's foot with his muzzle and nibbled his toes with his lips.

"Hee-haw," Taco neighed loudly, and Dante giggled and pumped his chubby arms and legs so enthusiastically that Frost had to tighten his grip on the boy. Frost and Zoey chuckled at the donkey's antics.

"He's got a strong kick," Frost said, turning the baby around to rest against his shoulder. "And I'm talking about Dante, not Taco, although I'm sure the donkey does, as well."

"Tell me about it," Zoey said with a groan. "I had to carry that boy for nine months. He'd jam his sharp little heels into my ribs until I was certain I was bruised from the inside. Ari, too. Sometimes I thought the both of them were doing gymnastics."

Again, a heaviness settled over Frost. He should have been there, supporting Zoey throughout her pregnancy. Experiencing the singular joy of feeling his babies' kicks while they were still in the womb. Taking Zoey to all her doctor's appointments and seeing the little beans' pictures on the ultrasound. Hearing the twins' heartbeats for the very first time. Finding out they were having a boy and a girl, maybe throwing a gender reveal party. Holding both of the twins in his arms when they were just newborn.

And that had just been the time up to when the babies were born. He'd also missed every milestone they'd made all the way up to four months, things he couldn't get back. He'd been robbed of all that, and he couldn't help the ire that rose from his thoughts, clouding his chest and his mind. Zoey was no less than a thief, having stolen what he was quickly coming to realize were his most precious gifts.

The more he thought about it, the angrier he became.

"Why don't you call and find out where your mom is and then let's go ahead and load up the sleigh," he suggested, knowing his tone was coming off harsh but unable—or unwilling—to explain why. "I'm in charge of setting up the bonfire, so we need to get there early."

Which was only partly true. It was his job to build the actual bonfire and light it, but his brother Sharpe would have already neatly stacked the wood and various kindling by the firepit. With the help of some handy lighter fluid, it would only take him a few minutes to get a blaze going.

Though it was a mild evening for winter in Colorado, most of his family were driving out to the bonfire, leaving the sleigh for those who wanted the experience of sleigh bells in the snow—in this case, Zoey. It had seemed like a good idea when he'd first thought of it, but now he couldn't fathom why he'd wanted to do something special for Zoey.

What had she ever done for him?

Nothing. That's what.

And it was all he could do not to respond with exactly the same attitude back at her.

Except Jesus had spoken of turning the other cheek. Of going two miles with Zoey when she was only demanding he go one.

To be truthful, though, she hadn't asked anything of him, and he realized he wished she had. He would have much preferred that she insisted he be the father he now wanted to be. Leaving the decision to him made him feel as if he was going to have to be proactive if he wanted to be involved in the twins' upbringing. His cheek was stinging with disillusionment for all he'd missed, and he didn't know how to forgive Zoey for that or to turn his face only to get slapped again.

He didn't know how to forgive, much less forget.

Zoey wrapped a wool blanket tightly around Ari and Dante, making sure they were warm. She was shivering as they sat on the back seat of the sleigh. Back when they'd first been dating, she would have sat in front next to Frost, her hand tucked through his arm. But now, he hadn't given her any choice in the matter, and maybe it was better that way. He'd simply and wordlessly helped her up onto the back seat and then strapped the babies into their car seats. He handed her a wool blanket, then got into the front seat and encouraged the Shires into motion.

She had imagined this moment so many times since she'd realized the twins were Frost's babies, but nothing could have prepared her for the stinging ice in Frost's tone and in his actions. For a short time there, it had seemed like he was going to be able to put their past behind him and move forward as things now were; but then, just as suddenly, a brick wall had gone up between them—so vivid and palpable it was almost physical. She wasn't sure what she'd said or done that had prompted the sudden change in his attitude, but she desperately wanted Frost to return to his usual gentle self.

She had a lot to account for. She knew it. And she knew it was her own fault things between them felt so uncomfortable and awkward. Perhaps someday she'd be able to share the whole story with him, but that day wasn't today, so she was going to have to do the best she could to dodge the shade Frost was throwing at her.

She was a study in opposites, and her stomach was tumbling with nerves. On one hand, the Winslow bonfires were some of her favorite memories ever. She was an only child, so interacting with the six Winslow siblings had always been a treat. Now, however, she'd be facing them as the woman who'd broken their brother's heart. She didn't know how much he'd shared with them, but she felt certain nothing he may have said would have been good.

As if that wasn't enough, it sounded as if there were quite a few additions since the last time she'd visited. It felt a little overwhelming, having to meet a bunch of new people in these frustrating circumstances. Would she have to explain herself to everyone?

And then there were the babies. How were the tight-knit Winslows going to take the news that she'd borne Frost's children without even letting him know they existed? The babies were Frost's siblings' new niece and nephew.

Again, a lot depended on how much Frost had shared with them—and in what way. Had he shared his anger and irritation with them? She imagined by now the whole family was already aware she was back in town with Frost's twins. Of course, they'd accept the twins. There was no doubt about that. But whether or not they'd accept *her* was a whole other story.

And oh, how desperately she wanted them to accept her the way they used to, back in the day.

She hadn't realized just how much until this moment. With the Winslows supporting them, she and Frost would hopefully be able to work through their issues and become the parents Dante and Ari needed. But if they turned her away and walled up behind their brother, she didn't know what she would do.

She didn't even have her mother there for support yet, though she would be arriving later in the evening with her violin. Her mom was someone who'd be on her side no matter what and was one of the few people in the world who knew the whole truth behind the story of why she'd turned down Frost's proposal. She knew she could trust her mother not to give away her secrets, even if Mom thought Zoey ought to share the whole truth with Frost.

Which she would.

One day.

Zoey turned her thoughts to her violin. At least she had that. She could express her emotions through music, no matter what else this night may deliver, whether good or bad, happy or sad, and even emotions like anger and frustration. She could capture all those feelings with her instrument.

It was going to be a busy night either way, she realized as Frost pulled the sleigh close to the bonfire area. There were already at least a dozen people there, everyone from Frost's elderly grandfather and his new wife down to toddlers playing around near their parents.

Zoey recognized many of the adults—Frost's brother Sharpe and sisters Ruby and Molly. She'd been previously introduced to Molly's husband and children, but she didn't yet see Felicity or Avery or their spouses. A dark-haired man had his arm possessively around Ruby, so Zoey mentally catalogued that knowledge, pairing the two up. That left a pretty ginger-haired woman as Sharpe's significant other. The preteen boy with the mop of red curls was no doubt related to this woman, and once again, Zoey mentally indexed the information, hoping against hope she'd be able to keep it all straight in her mind.

She'd been so worried about introducing the twins to the Winslows that she hadn't really thought about how much their group had grown and how many new people she'd be meeting today.

Zoey wasn't usually shy, but it felt as if the whole Winslow shindig had grown substantially since she'd last been here. It was more than a little overwhelming since all eyes would be on her—both those she knew and those to whom she'd be introduced.

"Zoey?"

She looked down to see that Frost was holding his arms up to her, his gaze questioning. Evidently while she was sitting in the sleigh woolgathering, he'd lit the bonfire, which was already turning into a snapping blaze.

"Sorry," she apologized, even though she wasn't exactly sure what she was apologizing for, other than not knowing how long he'd been standing there with his arms up, waiting to help her down.

"No worries. You want to hand me Dante first? I'll give him to whoever is most anxious to hold him first and then I'll come back for you and Ari. I can't wait to show the twins around."

He scooped Dante into his arms and turned toward his waiting family. "This chunky little fellow is my son, Dante," he said proudly, gently kissing the baby on top of his head. "Who wants first dibs at him?"

There was a mad scramble toward the baby, so much so that Zoey held her breath. It looked like a swarm of people surrounding the infant, and Zoey wondered again how she was going to get through this evening. Mostly, the men in the group held back and let the cooing women fight over who got to hold Dante first. Felicity won out, and she immediately curled the baby in her arms while a man, most likely her husband, looked on with a grin.

Joined by Zoey's mom, who'd arrived just after them, Frost immediately returned to the sleigh, passing Ari to her grandma and helping Zoey down with his other hand, curling his arm gently around her waist and easily lifting her to the ground. He might hate her now after all had been said and done, but that didn't stop him from being a perfect gentleman. But how could he be any less? She shouldn't have expected any less from him. Her whole life may have changed, but he was still the Frost she'd fallen in love with back in high school. The sensitive, caring man who'd made her heart work overtime every time they were together.

"Here's my beautiful daughter, Ari." Frost introduced the second baby, who was now back in his arms, to the group with another wide, joyful grin.

"How blessed can you be?" asked a burly fellow with a booming voice and a gleam of amusement sparkling from his blue eyes. Zoey remembered this man as Avery's husband Jake. "Babies are so fun at that age. Or at any age, really. And you've got two for the price of one."

Just as they had with Dante, the women swarmed around Frost, wanting to be the first to take baby Ari off his hands. Zoey hovered behind him, unsure of what to do or say, and feeling as if she were standing out like a stark, prickly weed in the midst of a fine field of colorful wildflowers.

Frost glanced over his shoulder and gestured Zoey to his side. "I'm sure most of you remember Zoey from back during my high school and college days when we were dating, but…well, yeah," he stammered before coming to a slow stop, apparently just as unable to explain their situation as she was. There weren't words for their current condition. "We haven't…er…seen each other in a while, but she is the twins' mother."

And that was all he said.

Chapter Four

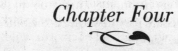

No judgment.

There could have been. Very possibly even there *should* have been. Frost definitely deserved a lecture, at the very least, for his part in having children out of wedlock. He'd broken not only with his own faith, but that of his family. But as he made a quick sweep of those gathered around him, all he saw was joy beaming from every face and genuine, supportive smiles all around.

Frost swallowed hard. Despite how hard he was on himself, he'd known this would be how his amazing siblings would react. To the Winslows, any baby was a blessing and a cause for celebration. No matter what circumstances had led to the birth of the twins, everyone still embraced them—and him.

Ever since they'd arrived at the bonfire, Dante and Ari had been passed around from one Winslow sibling to another, as if they were participating in some live-infant game of hot potatoes, with one small but critical change in the rules. Everyone wanted to *keep* the sweet, precious potatoes in their arms, not pass Dante or Ari on to the next person.

Frost realized he wasn't going to get a turn to hold his twins anytime soon, but he supposed that was the whole point of them being there at all and why he'd called his siblings to gather at the bonfire in the first place. He smiled and settled into his usual spot on a large tree stump. After opening his guitar case and pulling it out, he took a moment to tune it by ear before breaking into song, a familiar ancient hymn he could play underneath the mill of everyone's happy conversations.

He'd just started the second verse when Zoey joined him with the sweet, poignant strings of her violin.

Even though he'd been the one to suggest she bring her instrument to accompany him as she had back when they'd been dating, the sound of the violin surprised him so much that he nearly fell backward off his seat. He played a couple of off-sounding chords before he was able to pull himself together enough to join her again.

It had been so long since they'd played their instruments together. In some ways it felt like yesterday, and in other ways, it felt like forever. At one time in the not-so-distant past, he'd thought their magnificent harmonies, with both their stringed instruments and their voices, were part of why God had called them together as a couple. He'd believed they would minister together with their music all their lives.

The magnificent sound was still there between them, even if the relationship wasn't.

He paused when the song ended, glancing at Zoey and waiting for her to give him some guidance as to what she wanted to play next. She likewise hesitated and looked at him until their gazes locked and they shared an awkward laugh. It never used to be this uncomfortable between them.

Back when they'd first started dating, they'd been so

finely tuned with each other that they could segue from one song to the next without missing a single beat—even if the musical genres were widely ranged and diverse from song to song. They could play everything from country, to pop, to classical, to Broadway, to hymns and worship songs. Sometimes it was just Frost and Zoey playing and singing together, and sometimes the other Winslows joined in, creating amazing harmonies that always moved Frost's heart—the hymns and contemporary worship songs most especially.

Zoey lifted her bow and closed her eyes as she started one of her favorite classical pieces, and Frost delicately fingered the guitar chords to back her up. As always, she was spectacular, and as he'd already told her, he had no doubt she would rock her audition for the Colorado Symphony Orchestra. In his opinion, she probably ought to be given first chair, as her gift was so magnificent. He had no doubt she could do whatever she set her mind to, especially with her music, especially the CSO.

When she finished the classical piece, there wasn't a single sound around the bonfire other than the crackle and snap of the fire. Everyone was enrapt, even the babies, and it took a few moments for the group to shake themselves off enough to clap for Zoey. When the applause finally came, though, it was all whooping and laughing, as loud and rambunctious as only the Winslow clan could be.

Dante, who was currently sitting on Jake's lap, clapped his meaty hands with the help of the large man. Ari, on the other hand, who had been lulled into a sound sleep on Emma's lap while the music had been playing, was now jolted awake from the noise and promptly burst into frightened tears.

"Aww, did we accidentally scare you, baby girl?" Emma's husband Sharpe cooed, taking Ari from his wife and curling her onto his wide shoulder, gently patting her back to soothe and reassure her.

"I'll take her," said Frost, preparing to set his guitar aside for the sake of his child. In truth, he had no idea what to do with a crying baby, but Ari was his daughter, and so it was his responsibility to love and comfort her when she was upset. And if his edgy brother Sharpe could do it successfully, how hard could it be? His brother was hardly an expert with babies, although his wife Emma was currently four months pregnant with their first child.

But before he had the opportunity to put down his guitar, Zoey's mom waved him away, pulling a bottle out of a nearby zebra-patterned diaper bag and handing it to Sharpe.

"We've got things here under perfect control, hon. You and Zoey just keep playing your lovely songs together."

Frost caught Zoey's gaze and raised his eyebrows. The decision was hers to make as to whether or not to keep playing, as well as on the next song choice.

Zoey grinned and pointed her bow toward Emma's little brother Aidan and his tousled mop of red hair. "This one's for you," she told the preteen, and then promptly broke into the old Irish fiddling reel "Red-Haired Boy."

Frost quickly jumped in to accompany her, enjoying the opportunity to do a little more complex fingering on the strings as opposed to the simple chording he had been doing in previous songs. He marveled at how swiftly Zoey could switch from the most difficult classical pieces to fiddling an Irish reel with such joy and vibrancy that it got everyone from oldest to youngest on their feet dancing around the light of the bonfire.

How could it even be the same instrument—the violin and the fiddle? It was truly remarkable, the difference in the two sounds, and it was all about who held it in their hands. Frost was well aware of everything Zoey could do with her instrument, from Chopin and Bach to Irish folk songs and country jigs—without pausing a single beat in between them. He'd even seen her play an electric fiddle once at a concert, although she'd later admitted that it hadn't really been her thing, and she preferred the violin she'd grown up with. It had been a good experience for her, though, she'd told Frost, and she enjoyed it. She just preferred the nice, steady instrument she'd had for years.

Though she was wearing snow boots and not dancing shoes, Zoey moved over by Aidan and tapped out an Irish step around the boy without missing a single note, the beat going faster and faster as she danced and twirled. Aidan stood stock still while his cheeks turned a blooming pink that clashed with the red of his curly hair.

"The name of the song is 'Red-Haired Boy,'" Frost told Emma with a grin, still picking at his own instrument.

"Isn't that cool, Aidan, that someone wrote a song about you?" Emma asked with a bright smile. "My sweet, red-headed brother."

Frost smothered a chuckle, remembering how awkward and ungainly he'd felt when he was Aidan's age, and how mortified he would have been by all the attention he was currently receiving. Being a preteen boy, Aidan looked as if he wanted to dig a hole and disappear into it rather than have someone single him out and sing and dance around him.

Zoey switched to another familiar contemporary praise song and Frost's siblings and their spouses sang along, their voices remarkably harmonious as they broke into parts, everything from Jake's deep bass to Felicity's high, sweet soprano. To Frost, who lived for creating music both with his instrument and vocally, this was God at work. Sometimes it sounded as if there were even more voices joining in than he could count of the people present.

After quickly double-checking on where the twins were—currently curled up and sound asleep on Ruby's and Molly's laps—Frost took a deep, cleansing breath and added his own rich tenor to the mix of voices. What had started out as an anxiety-filled, difficult-to-take-a-breath evening was quickly turning into one he was genuinely enjoying. Gone were his tight muscles and deep frown; they were now replaced by feelings he couldn't even put into words.

It had been far too long since he and Zoey had accompanied each other on their instruments and joined their voices together. There was a time he'd believed this would never happen again.

Maybe, just maybe, the future wouldn't be so bad, after all.

He could only pray that sentiment might be true one day.

For a short while, Zoey had lost herself in playing her violin, joining in the jubilant music with Frost and his family and completely forgetting all the trials that had once taken her away from here. It felt so *right* to be sharing this bonfire and her music with the Winslows. She loved the opportunity to do a little joyful fiddling for a change, being able to just close her eyes and let go. Lately, it had been nothing but hours upon hours a day of serious classical violin work for her, as her audition for the CSO was quickly approaching.

She loved this evening so much. What a blessing it was turning out to be. Odd as it sounded, playing around the Winslow bonfire with the whole family present had been one of her favorite ways to spend dates with Frost back when they were together. Joy filled her heart as she remembered those old times…*before.*

She had to admit she'd been worried and embarrassed about facing the Winslows this evening. She used to be close to some of his sisters, but she hadn't talked to them in years. Not since she'd broken their brother's heart.

And as if that wasn't enough to make them all hate her, she'd suddenly shown up in town with Frost's babies— twins she hadn't even told him about until well after they were born.

They very well *could* have judged her the way she judged herself every moment of every day.

They could have. And as far as she was concerned, they *should* have. But they hadn't. She hadn't felt any of the ostracism or cold shoulders she'd expected. Instead, everyone in the Winslow clan, those she knew and those to whom she'd been newly introduced, had welcomed her—and Dante and Ari—with open arms. They'd joyfully passed around the babies to the point where she hadn't held either one of them even once since she'd arrived. Between their broods of children that spanned in age from newborns to preteens—no one could ever accuse any of Frost's siblings and their spouses of not loving kids.

These people, this bonfire…it felt as if she'd come home.

Out of nowhere, the happiness she'd been experiencing darkly clouded over in her chest like a sudden thunderstorm, lightning striking through her temples and behind her eyes. She was used to major migraines coming on quickly at times, but this one was different. Her heart clenched and then raced as if she were experiencing a heart attack, and she couldn't catch a breath. Her gaze darkened, spots appeared before her eyes, and for a moment she thought she might lose consciousness.

It had to be a migraine, as different as this one felt, perhaps something caused by anxiety. As if that wasn't bad enough, a genuine, physical panic attack was accompanying it. But her head didn't hurt nearly as bad as her heart.

She couldn't do this.

What had she been thinking?

"Oh," she sobbed under her breath, squeezing her eyes shut and clapping a hand over her mouth. With her other shaky hand, she hurriedly placed her violin in its case and snapped it closed. Without looking back for fear the others would see the tears streaming down her face, she headed straight for the tree line as fast as she could run, though she was hampered by the six inches of new snowfall.

"Zoey?" She heard Frost's voice coming from close behind her, and she quickened her pace. "Zoey? Honey? What happened? Are you okay?"

She didn't stop, even though she knew how easy it would be for Frost to catch up to her. It wasn't as if she could outrun him, even without the snow hampering her. He was a large man with equally huge strides compared to her. He could take one step to every two or three of hers.

Her breath came in short, painful gasps as the cold air stung her lungs. She scrambled forward, branches scratching her arms as if they were reaching for her, and roots she couldn't see through the snow threatened to trip her. Her boots slipped and skidded.

She couldn't think straight, and her heart pounded in her ears. She only knew she had to get away from the bonfire and the Winslows—just until she could pull herself together. Embarrassment flooded through her.

She glanced back to see if she could spot Frost chasing her.

Thud.

As she turned around, she suddenly ran into what at first felt like a solid brick wall—but the wall in question immediately surrounded her with strong, muscular arms and spoke in a familiar soft, tender voice.

Somehow, Frost had managed to get around her without her seeing him and had approached her from the front.

"Zoey?" Frost asked softly, gently stroking her hair. "Honey, what's wrong??"

A tremor ran through her. Her breath changed, and not just from her panicked running. She was positive Frost hadn't even realized he'd used his special term of endearment for her.

Twice now, he'd said it—once when she'd been running and now when he stopped her. Her heart twisted, more from emotion than physical exertion.

"Zoey?" he asked again in a whisper. "Talk to me."

She startled and pressed closer into his arms when a dog barked near her heel. She hadn't realized Daisy had been following her as well. The beagle put her front paws on Zoey's jeans and nuzzled her hand with her muzzle, her whole backside wiggling for attention.

"Daisy, no. Down." The dog immediately dropped to

the ground, her gaze on Frost as she waited for further commands.

Frost bent his head to speak to Zoey. "I'm so sorry. Daisy doesn't usually jump on people like that. I've trained her better. Not jumping on people is one of the first things all service dogs learn. But in her defense, dogs have a sixth sense about stuff like this. I think she's just worried about you. As am I—er, I mean, everyone at the bonfire," he stammered. "You just shot off like that and no one knew why."

"I'm sure Daisy can sense my anxiety," Zoey said, sighing as she reached down to scratch behind the beagle's ears.

Frost picked a twig from Zoey's hair and then gently brushed a stray lock back away from her face, curling it around her ear with the tips of his fingers so his gaze could better meet hers. She realized what a mess she must look right now, and she was glad Frost couldn't peer into her soul, because her insides were in even worse shape—a gray, snarled mess of emotions.

With another shaky breath, she pressed her hands into his chest and pushed away from him, turning so she didn't have to see the concern in his eyes. What possible reason could he have for caring about how she was feeling right now? She didn't deserve his attention. It was heartrending.

"What's going on, Zoey?"

Despite the thick wool peacoat she wore, she suddenly felt icy cold and shivered, wrapping her arms around herself in an unconsciously defensive gesture that Frost clearly noticed. He ignored the way she'd wrenched herself from his grasp and ran his large palms up and down her arms to warm her up.

"I don't know. I was feeling claustrophobic, and I suddenly couldn't catch a breath," she admitted, knowing even as she said it how ridiculous it sounded, especially with the unspoken words *to save my life* punctuating the end. Stupid panic attacks. She hadn't had them until after that night in the dorms, and she had no reason to have one now.

With the exception of a few of the new spouses, the Winslows were people she had known all her life. And the bonfire was located in the open woods with a broad starlight night above them and fresh winter air to pull into her lungs.

How could she possibly feel claustrophobic in such circumstances?

But it wasn't about *where* she was, or even *with whom*. It was *when* she was.

It was *time*, like a deadly vise on her throat—then and now, the woman she'd once been versus the person she was now.

Before and after.

"I just can't handle this right now," she admitted bluntly, turning back toward him and shrugging, as if running off into the forest in the dark of night was no big deal. She lifted her chin. "There are just too many people. And while I enjoyed playing music with you again tonight, it's just… too much for me. I'm afraid I'm going to have to skip out."

As if she hadn't already skipped out. She wanted to perish from embarrassment just thinking about how she must have looked to the others.

"Would you mind asking my mom to bring the babies out to the parking lot so I can go home?" she asked, unable to look him in the eye. She was such a chicken, un-

able even to return to the group to pick up the twins. She'd
be clucking soon at this rate.

"I—okay. If that's what you want." He narrowed his
eyes and reached for her arm, but she jerked away once
again and stepped out of his reach. "Are you sure you're
going to be okay?" he asked again. "You've ripped your
jacket."

She glanced down to find he was right. She'd dashed
off in such a wave of panic that she'd ignored the branches
grasping at her with their long, sharp, fingerlike limbs,
and they'd done considerable damage to one of her sleeves.

She pressed her fingers to her still-throbbing temples.
Frost looked as if he wanted to reach out to her again, but
instead he stuffed his fists into the pockets of his wool-
lined jean jacket and shifted from one foot to the other.
He probably didn't want to be rejected again, not that she
could blame him.

She was getting good at rejecting him, and she de-
spised herself for it.

There was a time when Frost would have soothed her
migraine with his gentle fingers massaging her temples
and the rich tenor of his voice as he spoke tenderly to her.

But she'd ruined that, and she realized with a pain in
her heart that rivaled the one in her head that this was
now her new reality. Period. She couldn't go back to the
way things had been, no matter how much she wanted to
do so. She'd ruined everything—not just with Frost, but
with his family as well.

They would never *act* as if anything had changed, of
course—not to her face, anyway. But the truth was, *everything* had changed.

She would eventually have to come to terms with the

way things were now and learn how to live within this new reality.

But not tonight.

Tonight, she would flee from all the emotions overwhelming her, go home, put the twins down for the night and hide away under the covers of her own bed. Only then would she allow herself to give in and cry her eyes out.

She knew she was acting cowardly, but she couldn't bring herself to return to the bonfire where everyone's curious, if caring, gazes would be waiting.

"Tell my mom I'll wait for her in her car, okay?" She knew her mother had driven to the area just outside the bonfire, so it wasn't much of a walk.

His lips grew tight, but he nodded. "Sure. Whatever you need."

"Oh—and don't forget my violin, if you don't mind grabbing it."

"Of course. No problem at all." He paused. "There's no moon tonight. Let me walk you to the car."

She shook her head. "Thanks, but I know the way, even in the dark." After all, she lived in the dark these days, or at least her heart did.

He tilted his head and observed her for a moment before turning toward the bonfire with a sigh. He started to walk away with Daisy at his heel, but then he stopped and pointed the beagle back in Zoey's direction.

"Stay with Zoey," he commanded firmly.

Zoey had no idea how Daisy could understand such a confusing instruction. It wasn't as if it would have been in the list of commands she'd have learned. But apparently Daisy was an exceptionally bright puppy who understood human language, or at least human emotions, because she immediately turned and trotted to Zoey's heel.

For a reason Zoey couldn't fathom, much less explain, the dog's presence reassured her. She couldn't believe what a difference it made. It was no wonder Daisy was training to be a service dog.

Tonight, Zoey was the person who needed help.

She wasn't alone in the dark.

Chapter Five

Feeling lost and not knowing what to do about his relationship with Zoey, if one could even call it a relationship, Frost visited church on Monday afternoon just to spend some quiet time with Jesus and offer up all his problems to the Lord. He'd attended the service the day before as he always did, but he hadn't been able to find the peace he needed, with all his friends and neighbors milling around. He'd stayed in the sanctuary to pray after the service and no one had interrupted him, but he could hear the clamor of voices coming from the nearby fellowship hall and hadn't been able to focus his thoughts and his heart.

Usually, his prayer time came during his daily job of caring for the farm and all the animals, which he considered all of God's creatures. Frost often kept a running conversation going with his Maker as he worked, but right now he felt as if he needed a little more than what his usual prayer life offered. He needed increased focus and intent, which he hoped this visit to the church would help him find.

He was clueless as to what to do about Zoey, how to help her through whatever it was she was struggling with right now.

He didn't know how to move forward with his own life, either, for that matter. So much had changed in so little time. It boggled his mind, and that was nothing to say of the mixed-up state of his emotions.

Inside the church's silent sanctuary, he slipped to his knees and quieted his mind as he pondered the very great sacrifice God the Father had made on his behalf in sending His only Son to save him.

This meant a whole different thing now that Frost was a father with a son and daughter of his own. His understanding of such sacrifice had grown exponentially since getting to know the twins. What great love God had for him, despite all the knots he'd managed to create in his life. He couldn't even fathom it.

As for his own future, he already knew what sacrifices he would be called to make, and he was prepared to step forward in faith. He'd intended to go to college and get a degree in teaching music, so he wasn't just the guy who played guitar and sang on open mic night every Friday at Sally's Pizza. Not anymore. He once had the desire to spread his love of music to others. In particular, he wanted to work with children.

Sure, he had a few private guitar students, both children and adults, but he'd been dreaming of so much more. It didn't do him any good to have a decent voice if he didn't know how to translate that knowledge to his students. The old adage that the best vocal teachers had vocal teachers was true. He'd never had a lesson in his life, so how could he hope to teach others?

And that was nothing to say of what he'd need to learn to step into an elementary or middle school music teacher position and direct the band and choir. At the moment, that was way beyond his knowledge and experience.

He'd even finished writing the essay on his college entrance application, though he didn't think it was very good, as his writing skills were rusty. He still had a few things to finish on the application, but now the point seemed moot.

This wasn't the first time he'd put his dreams on hold. He wasn't able to attend college with Zoey as they'd originally planned because there were family issues in his household that had kept him from leaving. During his senior year of high school, a drought had hit the farm's coffers hard. He wasn't resentful that his life had happened that way, although he did sometimes wonder how different things would have been had he been able to attend college with Zoey. They would have been better able to maintain their relationship at college together instead of long distance, and maybe things wouldn't have ended the way they had.

Perhaps it was better if he just put his teaching dreams away for good this time and focused on his future at the farm and being a father to the twins.

Is that what You're trying to tell me, Lord? That I should give up on my dreams? That You've got a different plan for me?

He made a decent living from the Christmas tree farm and knew his siblings appreciated the work he did with the animals. He'd been able to tuck away money for college, putting every spare cent he'd made into savings. That money could now be used to take care of his babies, he supposed.

He'd already experienced his first major shock regard-

ing the kind of money required to equip a baby layette—
much less buying two of everything. And his son and
daughter deserved the very best. He would want to start
putting away money for their college expenses, too, so it
would have time to accumulate interest. He could never
start too early on that. He wanted his children to be able
to do and be whatever they wanted to be when they grew
up, even if they wanted to be a doctor or a lawyer, or anything else that took many extra years of schooling. He'd
missed the first few months of their lives; he vowed he
would be there to help for the rest of their years.

And he was sure there were plenty of other things he
was missing. These were all things he needed to discuss
with Zoey, he realized. She would have a better idea of
what he needed to do as a new father, help him get his
head on straight. But it almost felt as if she'd iced him out
Saturday night, building a wall so high between them that
he would never be able to break it down.

As if she had any right to do that. If anything, he should
be the one pushing her away, though given the circumstances he could never do that.

But then he gazed up at the cross of Christ and his heart
broke anew. A single tear ran down his cheek.

The Apostle Peter's words sprang into his mind. *"Lord,
if my brother sins against me, how often must I forgive
him? As many as seven times?"* And Jesus's kind, thoughtful answer that squeezed Frost's heart and made his chest
tighten. *"I say to you, not seven times but seventy-seven
times."*

In other words, he had to find a way to get past his pain
so he could effectively co-parent with Zoey. Frost fisted
his hands and cringed. This was going to be the hardest

thing he'd ever done in his life, forgiving Zoey for breaking his heart. If it weren't for the twins—

But it *was* about his babies.

And that changed everything.

At that moment, in the quiet of the church, on his knees before the Lord, he knew it was up to him to take the first step forward—toward reconciliation.

Toward peace.

Zoey had to admit she was surprised when she heard from Frost on Tuesday evening after the way she'd cut and run Saturday night. They made plans to meet together on Wednesday afternoon. She didn't blame him for not reaching out on Sunday or Monday. After the way she'd treated him at the bonfire, it was a wonder he wanted to spend any time with her at all.

Of course, it really wasn't about her, though, was it? He didn't want to spend time with her. He wanted to spend more quality time getting to know Dante and Ari.

Wednesday was a nice day as Colorado winter weather was concerned, and the sun was shining, so they were going forward with the walk he'd suggested across part of the Winslow's vast acreage. Just in case, before placing them in their car seats, Zoey layered the twins in long sleeves, fleece jackets, and cute animal beanies—a kitten for Ari and a panda for Dante—complete with earflaps and pom-poms to warm their heads.

They intended to take a long stroll around a lovely lake that was open for ice skaters on weekends this time of year. In the summer, Frost and Sharpe stocked it full of rainbow trout so kids would be sure to catch a fish with poles they rented from the farm.

Thanks to the work and sacrifices made by all six Winslow siblings, the farm was flourishing and getting better every year. She was impressed by their accomplishments and proud of all of them, especially Frost. She knew how much he'd sacrificed in his own life for the sake of his family. She knew he'd wanted to go to college with her but had been held back by the drought. And now she'd given him the additional burden of becoming a father—not that he would ever think of his babies as burdens, no matter how overwhelmed he must be feeling right now. No—to Frost, Dante and Ari were blessings.

Zoey pulled her white SUV into the farm parking lot and chose a space. Frost was already waiting, looking especially good in his usual wool-lined jean jacket, blue jeans, tan cowboy hat and well-worn tan cowboy boots. Daisy was sniffing around near him, close enough to be by his side but distracted by nearby scents.

Their eyes met as she turned off her engine and her stomach did a little flip. With an audible sigh, she clamped down the feeling as soon as it rose, knowing nothing good could come of it. It didn't matter how handsome he was or how his charming, boyish good looks and silver-blue eyes could melt butter.

That ship had sailed a long time ago, and this was a whole new thing entirely. She had to learn how to deal—and fast.

Frost opened the back door next to Ari.

"How do you work this thing?" Frost asked, fiddling with the buckle of Ari's car seat while Zoey pulled out the double stroller from the back and unfolded it.

"Ah, the car seat. One of the first major painful parental learning curves—after labor and delivery, that is."

The moment the words were out of her mouth, she wished them back as Frost's eyes iced over, no doubt thinking about how he'd missed her whole pregnancy and the major event of their babies being born because of her.

"I'm sorry," she immediately said, the words tumbling from her mouth. "I only meant—"

"I know what you meant," he snapped back, cutting her off. "Now, are you going to show me how this gadget works, or does poor Ari just have to sit here while I figure it out myself?"

Wow.

The emotional weather had just gone from sunny to an ice storm.

Despite his name, it was so *not* like Frost to bark at her that way. But she reminded herself to give him grace. She couldn't imagine what he must be going through right now.

"Unbuckle the shoulder harness and then push the big yellow button to unlock it. You'll have to unthread her arms to get her out."

"Yeah, I've got her," he said, pulling Ari out and planting little kisses on her chubby cheek. "How are you doing, sweet little miss?" he crooned in a voice that made Zoey's heart flip over.

Zoey was busy trying to release a squirming, uncooperative Dante from his car seat when Frost whooped.

"What?" she asked in alarm.

"She smiled at me," he exclaimed, puffing up like a rooster and displaying the widest grin she'd ever seen on him. But just as quickly, he deflated. "Or is it just gas or something? I heard babies can't really smile at first."

Zoey held up a hand, cutting short his words. "It was

a genuine smile. She loves kisses, and your beard tickles her. Listen for her giggle. It's adorable. And I think she already knows you are someone special to her." Seeing the glow on Frost's face, she added her own smile. "Let's get these two into the stroller. You want to push?"

She hoped he could see she was making a genuine effort to co-parent with him. She couldn't change the past but she could make today shine like the sun, if only he'd let her.

Silently, she said what was almost a prayer—it would have been if she still believed God listened to her, which she didn't. God, if He was there at all, had abandoned her that night in the dorm when she'd needed Him most. He'd turned His gaze away and had let the unthinkable happen.

With effort, she turned her attention back to the present, knowing it did her no good to dwell on the past.

She tucked their Gram-made crocheted blankies securely around each baby and walked toward the lake in what Zoey hoped was a companionable silence. Her head was spinning with a million questions. They had so many things to discuss that she didn't know where to start.

Though the Winslows regularly blew the snow from the paths and kept them in good shape for visitors, just as they reached the path leading around the lake, Zoey slipped, and her feet went out from under her. She'd been so preoccupied thinking about the man beside her that she'd accidentally stepped on a patch of black ice. She knew the moment her boots touched the ice that she was out of control and going down.

She made a small squeak of distress and her arms flailed. She braced for impact, knowing it was going to be a hard one, leaving bruises at the least or worse—a sprained ankle or broken wrist.

Suddenly, Frost's arm curled around her waist, strong and steady.

With one hand firmly gripping the stroller and his booted feet carefully straddling the patch of black ice, Frost pulled her tightly to his side. She instinctively wrapped her arms around his neck for stability, but when their eyes met and locked, the moment became something else entirely.

How many times had they stood in just this way, enjoying each other's closeness as they moved through life together as a couple? Why had she taken her time with Frost for granted, assuming it would always be that way?

His gaze dropped to her lips, and she knew he was thinking the same thing.

But that was the past, and this was the present—and she couldn't let what felt like the inevitable happen.

With every bit of her strength, she stepped away from him, careful to avoid the patch of black ice.

"Well, thank you for the quick save," she quipped, adjusting the thick purple scarf around her neck that suddenly felt as if it were strangling her. "I obviously need to pay more attention to where I'm walking. You'd think I was new to the snow instead of being Colorado born and bred."

He just stood staring at her for a long, uncomfortable second before shrugging and turning his attention back to the twins.

After what felt like minutes but was probably only seconds, he glanced back at her, poised to speak, but then the moment passed.

Zoey felt a gaping hole in her heart, as if she'd just missed something important and would never get it back again.

How long would she feel this aching loss?

Chapter Six

Frost was struggling internally, though he was trying not to show his emotions on the outside. Holding Zoey in his arms, even for just those few short minutes, had made his heart roar to life.

Who was he kidding, thinking he no longer had feelings for Zoey?

Dante interrupted Frost's thoughts with a wail.

"What do you need, buddy?" he asked his son, but his gaze was on Zoey. Frost didn't yet know what the different crying sounds Dante and Ari made meant, though he hoped it wouldn't take him long to learn.

She smiled and shook her head.

"Hungry? Wet? Grouchy? Teething?" he suggested.

"Maybe all of the above. Could be none. Sometimes he just likes to holler for the sake of hollering."

"Hmm." An idea popped into his head and he reached forward to scrub a palm over his son's curly blond hair. "Ready to race, big guy? Think we can beat the doggy?" Ari was napping, so he only addressed his question to the still-crying Dante.

"Come race with us, Daisy. On your mark, get set… go!" He took off at a careful jog along the bumpy path, to his son's sheer delight. Daisy bounded along at his side, her large ears flopping as she barked her enthusiasm. Dante's wail turned into a delighted squeal, and he pumped his chunky arms and legs, completely forgetting what he'd been crying about.

"Be careful on the ice," Zoey called after him, which only caused Frost to grin even wider. He made race car sounds, to his son's delight. For the first time since the twins had come into his life, he felt like a genuine father—doing a dad thing like racing a stroller, while Mommy Zoey was reminding him to be safe with the kids.

After another minute or so, laughter bubbling from his lungs, which were stinging from the cold air, he slowed his pace and waited for Zoey to catch up. Both babies were now sound asleep, having been rocked by the steady movement of the stroller as he jogged.

"That was fun," he told Zoey with a wink.

Zoey pressed a hand to her chest. "Says you. I almost had a heart attack watching you scurrying around with the stroller. Crazy man."

"You know I would never put the twins in any danger."

"Of course not. I couldn't wish for a better daddy for Dante and Ari than you." Her voice tightened.

He narrowed his gaze on her. "What's that supposed to mean?"

A better daddy as opposed to whom? It wasn't the first time she'd alluded that there had been some question about the paternity of the twins. Was there another man in her life? He hadn't thought to ask.

"N-nothing," she stammered. "I just meant I always knew you'd be a good father. Even when we were first dating, I thought you'd be a great dad to your children. You know, house with a white picket fence, playing ball with the kids in the yard."

Which brought them straight back to the beginning. His muscles stiffened and he gripped the stroller with tight fists.

"Then why didn't you want me to be with you when you found out you were pregnant with my babies? I don't get it. You had to know I could have—*would* have—helped you and the twins from the very beginning."

There was a long, painful pause as Zoey clearly struggled with how to answer what should have been a simple question. He could see her wrestling with a dilemma in her expression. Finally, she drew in an audible breath, her words coming out in a rush.

"Because I didn't know whether or not they were yours."

Her words hit him so hard, it was all he could do not to drop to his knees in the snow, grasping at his stomach. It was as if all the air had been knocked from his lungs.

"What?" His voice came out an octave higher than usual.

Scrubbing a hand through his curls, his head pounded and his thoughts raced.

Always aware of her people, Daisy nudged her muzzle underneath Frost's hand, and he absently stroked her neck as he considered this new information.

"Were you that angry with me for what I'd done? Was this guy some kind of a rebound thing?"

Zoey burst into fiery, angry tears and shoved his shoulder hard. "How can you even say that? You know how I felt about you back then."

"Evidently, I had no clue whatsoever," he snapped back.

"I thought we were in love, but clearly, we weren't. Why don't you explain it to me." He knew he was hurting her with his words, but he couldn't help it. He was in so much pain from what she'd relayed to him with the power of a sharp lance, and he wanted her to feel the pain he did. All the emotions he thought he'd worked through after she'd rejected his proposal came rushing back as if they'd never left.

And now he was trying to process this new information, and it was just too much for his heart to handle.

Daisy perked her ears up, alerted by what was going on as she walked back and forth between them with a series of concerned whines and howls. She sensed the tension but wasn't sure who needed her comfort the most.

"It's okay, girl," he promised his dog, even though everything was definitely *not* okay. He took a few deep, calming breaths before asking, "When did you finally know Dante and Ari were mine? Because I get why you may not have wanted to tell me about the other man, but I still think you should have reached out to me, maybe asked me for a DNA test—*before* the twins were born."

"It's more complicated than that," she offered as her only explanation. He waited, but she didn't continue.

Ari woke up from the shrill sound of their voices and promptly burst into tears. Despite the tension displayed across her own face, Zoey immediately attended to the baby, taking Ari from the stroller and settling her on her shoulder, rocking her back and forth and making calm, shushing noises.

Whoever else Zoey was, whatever she'd done, she was a good mother. And that was maybe what confused Frost most of all.

Because it could have been different. It could—*should* have been a happily ever after between them. And their babies.

Now it wasn't, and it probably never could be.

He always thought he'd been the one who'd wrecked everything between them, but now he was beginning to see there was a much bigger picture he'd been missing.

Part of him wanted to ask for details: *Who was the guy? When had it happened? Before or after he'd proposed? Was that why she'd said no?*

Did what had happened between Zoey and this guy mean anything, or had she just been in a state of rebound, looking for any man who was not Frost? But if that was the case, she wouldn't have kept the other guy a secret, would she?

He opened his mouth to ask the questions, but no sound emerged from his lips.

The truth was, he didn't really want to know.

Zoey wasn't sure what to do now that Frost's emotional wall had gone up. This wasn't how she'd expected—or at least hoped—the day to go at all. She'd wanted them to be able to talk about the future, not the past. But she heard his voice harden the moment he became closed off, and she doubted she would be able to turn things around.

Daisy had evidently decided Zoey was the one who needed the most attention and was standing in front of her, her head and tail erect as she looked up, her huge brown eyes and a lolling tongue conveying doggy concern.

"It's okay, girl," Zoey assured the pup, gently patting her head. The dog obviously didn't buy it, and neither, for that matter, did Zoey. Nothing about this was *okay.*

She knew he had questions to which he rightfully needed and deserved answers, but try as she might, that story was still too fresh, even after all this time. And though she knew she could trust Frost with that knowledge, it would be a burden on him she just couldn't yet share.

"I had hoped," she said, stopping to swallow hard through her dry throat, "that we might be able to talk about practical stuff. With the babies, I mean." She cringed inwardly. That didn't sound reasonable even to her, not after what she'd just hit him with.

So, she was surprised when he said, "Okay."

"I mean, I thought we...*okay*?" She skidded to a verbal halt.

"Yeah. We have a lot to decide. I figured we'd talk first and then maybe visit Liam Wentworth for advice to help us sort out all the details of how I can help support the twins financially, and maybe get a couple of college investment accounts set up."

Liam was the town's best financial planner. Zoey wasn't surprised that Frost wanted to look into college funds for Dante and Ari, especially since it was lack of funds that had kept Frost from attending university right out of high school. He would want his children to have the opportunities he didn't have.

Frost nodded for them to keep walking. Ari was wide awake but calm, so Zoey put her back in the stroller and took over pushing it.

"We can do this without going to court over custody, right?" Frost asked, his voice tight and thready.

"Court?" Zoey exclaimed, her gaze widening. She hadn't even thought about the possibility of needing to get the government involved, or even a mediator. "Definitely not, Frost. When I came here and brought your children to you, it was with the full knowledge that you would want to be involved in their lives in a big way. As I mentioned earlier, I want your name to be on their birth certificates as their father, and I really hope you'll play a major role in their lives. They need the kind of good male role model only you can provide. We don't need a court to help us make future plans."

"I do think it would be a good idea to loop Liam into this," Frost said, having evidently regained his composure. Daisy pawed at his jeans, and he leaned down to scratch her ears. "You're right, though. Between the two of us, we can work out who has the babies when and try to cooperate with each other. In the long run, we need to be there for each other whenever we have issues or crises that need to be dealt with. Our families can help us out with that, as well. But I have a few financial questions I need answered—college tax-related funds and the like. And we need to start some kind of account that you can draw on when you need money for the twins' expenses."

"I don't want to take your money. That's not what this is about, and it never has been. Whenever you have the kids, you can spend your own money on them. And when I have them, likewise," she protested.

"While that sounds great in theory, do you really believe we'll be doing fifty-fifty childcare? Because if not, you'll be spending more on the twins than I will."

He had a point.

"So, it seems to me the first thing to do is figure out how we want to share the children. I've got plenty of time right now and can watch them twenty-four/seven, but if I get into the symphony—"

"When," he interrupted.

"If I get into the symphony," she repeated, "that'll be a whole other thing. I'll have a full-time practice schedule and all new decisions to make then. To be honest, I'm not even sure where I'll live."

Frost tucked his hands into the pockets of his jean jacket and turned around so he was walking backward in front of her and, for what seemed like the first time that day, he met her gaze.

She wondered what he saw when he looked at her. Probably much like what she saw in Frost's eyes—sadness. Confusion.

"I wish I had a solid answer for you about my future plans," she said. "But at this point, I don't."

"I know."

"But I feel as if you're pressuring me, like you've already made up your mind as to what I should do, despite everything that's still up in the air in my life."

"I know what I'd like to see happen, but that isn't up to me. As you said, we'll have to work it out when the time comes." He let out an audible breath. "But Zoey?"

"Hmm?"

"No matter what, it's all about the kids, right? We'll work on our relationship for their sakes?"

Daisy was at Zoey's heel, nudging and snuffling at her jeans. She leaned down to pat the dog's back.

"Without question," she promised him, all the while her heart was aching that it was no longer about the two of them.

If only...

She crouched and buried her face in Daisy's soft fur.

Oddly enough, the dog's presence calmed Zoey's heart and made her feel better—at least a little bit.

"You're such a sweetheart, aren't you?"

Ba-rooowww! Daisy howled as if in answer.

"She's working," Frost said, surprise lining his voice.

"What?"

"Just like earlier. I noticed she was alerting when you—well…when you were talking about…" His sentence dropped to a halt. "Zoey?"

She froze, half afraid of what he was going to say next. Had Daisy somehow helped him figure out that all wasn't as it seemed?

"I think you should come with me next week."

She hesitated. What was he talking about? "Where?"

"To court."

"Court? No—I thought we decided we didn't need to—"

"Not about the twins," he reassured her. "Daisy has a client we're going to meet with."

"Daisy? Not you?" She couldn't help the chuckle that escaped her lips at the thought of a beagle having a legal appointment.

Frost smiled. "A young teenage girl. I'd like you to watch how Daisy works. It's truly a sight to see."

She had to admit she was interested. She'd already experienced what Daisy could do on a limited basis in her own life, offering her acceptance and a calming presence when things felt out of control. She thought she understood what Frost meant about her being an emotional support animal, but she couldn't imagine what it would be like to really see Daisy in action in court.

But that would require spending additional time with Frost, which after today felt like it would be an ordeal.

On the other hand, they had to learn to work out a way to be cordial with each other for the sake of the twins.

"Okay," she said, jumping in before she could talk herself out of it. "Text me the details and let's do this."

Chapter Seven

Frost was proud of the work he was doing with Daisy. She'd come far in the past year, after he'd rescued her as a young mama from horrible circumstances and nursed her back to health. But that wasn't the reason he invited Zoey to accompany him to court—or not the whole reason, anyway.

The haze of anger and hurt when Zoey had admitted he hadn't been the only man in her life had him seeing red. For all he knew, she could still be dating the other guy, since they hadn't really gotten that far in a discussion about that. Yet, when she'd divulged she'd thought the twins were possibly not his, when they were walking around the lake the other day, Frost had noticed something.

Daisy.

He'd been in his own head, but he'd also been working many months with Daisy, closely observing every tell from the way her tail stiffened upward to the way her long, floppy ears pricked forward as if she was intently listening. And at the lake, she'd definitely been alerting—on Zoey.

Which meant Zoey wasn't telling him something—something deep and emotional. Yes, they'd been arguing at the time, so both of them had their hackles up. It could've been just that she was upset at having to admit that Frost hadn't been the only man in her life, but as upset as he clearly was about that, he didn't think that was what had caught Daisy's attention.

What wasn't Zoey telling him?

With Daisy's help, he was determined to find out.

"Ready to go?" he asked Daisy as he slipped on his silver suit jacket and straightened his royal blue tie. He took another look in the mirror and tousled his curly hair that could not be tamed by any brush or product.

Daisy howled her impatience. There was no cuter howl than a beagle's, which was part of the reason he'd chosen Daisy from a program that rescued dogs from puppy mills. Though she was still quite young, Daisy was a three-time mama. What had really drawn Frost to her was her drive and strength to live. Despite her terrible living conditions, she had a fighting spirit and still showed affection when Frost had reached out to her. A dog's ability to forgive humans was amazing; he could learn a lot from Daisy.

They'd been inseparable ever since, and not just because he was committed to their new service dog program to help victims of crimes, though there was that.

But the relationship between Frost and Daisy went beyond words. Deeper. She was at his heel day in and day out, living in his house and sleeping at the foot of his bed.

Which is why, he thought, he'd so quickly picked up Daisy's alert when she was with Zoey. As caught up as he'd been in his own emotions, he could easily have missed it, but he and Daisy worked as a team.

That was why he was so eager for Zoey to see what Daisy could do in court. Because eventually, when he confronted Zoey about what was really happening in her heart—and he would, sooner rather than later—she'd understand why he was asking. It was how he planned on opening that tough conversation—by pointing out how Daisy could sense it beyond what he as a man could intuit.

Ten minutes later, his mind still reeling with his thoughts, he was in front of Zoey's mom's house. He had driven his blue SUV instead of the black truck he preferred to drive, due to the price and quantity of gas it would take to go to Denver and back again. His truck was a real guzzler, and with the price of gas being what it was, it made more sense to drive the SUV. He supposed he also looked a bit more professional than he would in a beat-up, dusty work vehicle.

Zoey was waiting for him on her mother's porch, sitting on the stairs with her chin in her hand, looking thoughtful and maybe a little anxious.

He hopped out and ran around to the passenger side of the SUV as she approached, opening the door for her and holding out his hand to steady her.

"Wow. You look handsome today," she said, running an admiring glance over his suit. It was a far cry from his usual clothing, so it wasn't a huge surprise that she'd noticed, but that didn't stop his ego from inflating like a hot air balloon. At this point he would take whatever he could get, especially from Zoey.

"You're looking pretty good yourself." She was dressed head to toe in black, from her black slacks and frilly blouse to her fitted jacket and patent leather heels.

"Not too much black?" she asked, wrinkling her nose. "I didn't bother unpacking a lot since I don't yet know my future plans, so I'm pretty much living out of a suitcase right now. I mostly took out my casual clothes—jeans and sweaters—for Whispering Pines, with this one exception. This is my auditioning outfit."

"Well, it looks nice. If fancy clothes win auditions, you'll have it in the bag. Not that there's any question about that, anyway."

He couldn't help but grin when her cheeks reddened. Despite everything, he could still get to her, just as he'd been able to do back when they were first dating. Which meant nothing, but he enjoyed the moment anyway. He was cheesing big time and he didn't know why, but he just couldn't keep the smile off his face. Maybe today would be a good day.

As they drove down to Denver, Frost filled Zoey in on what they'd encounter when they got to court so she wouldn't be surprised or shocked by what she saw.

"We'll start in a private room at the court where we'll meet Peyton, a twenty-two-year-old young woman who was robbed at gunpoint. The thief was caught, and now she'll have to act as a witness and point him out to the court."

"That's frightening. I can't even imagine."

"I know. If it wasn't bad enough that she had to look down the barrel of a gun the first time, the defense is calling on her to testify. She initially didn't want to do it, but her lawyers have convinced her it's the best way for her to win her case."

"The defense? Why would they put her on the stand? Can they even do that?"

"I'm not sure why the defense would subpoena her. It doesn't make sense to me. But Peyton is moving forward with her lawyers' advice. She's a strong young woman seeking closure."

"You keep saying *young woman* as if you're way older than her," Zoey pointed out with a laugh. "You're not exactly an old man."

"I know, right? I guess that's just my way of distancing myself emotionally from Peyton and the situation she's facing. If I don't, I'll get too invested in her and her case."

She reached across and laid a comforting hand on his forearm. "We have to let the justice system work, right? Isn't that the whole point of what you're doing here?"

He blew out a breath to calm his nerves, which were sparking as much from Zoey's gentle touch as they were in anger at the kind of man who would hold an innocent woman at gunpoint.

"She had just closed the store and dimmed the lights so people would know not to enter. She had locked the door not realizing Dawson was still in the facility. When he approached her, he caught her entirely off-guard. She had a gun pointed directly at her face, so of course she would have been panicking. I think the defense is going to try to argue that she couldn't know for certain beyond a reasonable doubt who was holding the gun because she was staring down the barrel. In my mind, that's all they've got, or else why would they use it? Isn't that backward? I've never heard of anything like it. To me, it seems too dangerous a play to use, but I'm not a lawyer."

"But *does* she actually know what he looks like? Enough to vow to it in court under oath? I mean, as you said, the circumstances would have been working against her."

"Oh, yeah. She knows exactly who he is and can easily

point him out in court under oath. The night it happened, she worked with a police artist to create a portrait *and* she picked him out of a lineup several days later. That's why it doesn't make sense to me that the defense would call her onto the stand. If you ask me, the defense must be desperate. Dawson used weapons to rob convenience stores all up and down the I-25 corridor and crossed state lines, which is what made it a federal case. The ATF doesn't mess around. As far as I can tell, it's open-and-shut, unless they can intimidate her while she's on the stand."

"That sounds awful."

"I know. The defense lawyers will probably do their best to confuse her with their questioning. That's why we're going in today before the prosecution rests its case and the defense starts in on theirs. Peyton's lawyers want her to have time to practice with Daisy by her side, to help her feel the kind of pressure the defense may bring put on her and how to use the Daisy to help her concentrate on what must be done to win the trial. They want her to be prepared for the worst and be ready to speak up when the time comes."

"I'm sure Daisy will be a big help."

"Exactly. There's no question about that, which is what's so exciting to me about the canine therapy I'm pursuing now in the court system. Science has proven dogs can physically calm a person down and lower their blood pressure, not to mention focus their minds. I think you'll be amazed when you see what Daisy can do for Peyton."

And, he thought, he'd also have the opportunity to see Zoey's response to everything going on and get her thoughts about his work there. He was proud of that.

Yet, that wasn't the only reason he'd brought her today. He also wanted to see Zoey's reaction to the pressure she'd see today—and recognize Daisy's alert to her, if any.

Because if he was right, there was a lot that Zoey wasn't telling him. And Daisy would hopefully give him vital clues he needed to sniff out the truth so he could help Zoey if he could.

Zoey's stomach was churning by the time they reached the federal courthouse in Denver. Her experience at the dorm in Greeley was not at all comparable to Peyton's experience, but the feelings were the same—the helplessness. The panic. The fear.

She almost wished she could go back and discover the truth about who'd drugged her drink—and what had happened after that, if anything—so she could find the kind of closure Peyton sought in the courtroom today. She wouldn't tell Frost this, but she understood why Peyton was willing to face down the bad guy and point her finger at him.

Frost removed Daisy from her kennel in the back of the SUV and the dog immediately ran to Zoey, lolling her tongue and cocking her head to the side as if in question, followed by a sound that was halfway between a bark and a howl.

"Hey, you," Frost said, following the dog around with the red vest that indicated Daisy was a service animal. "At least wait until I put your vest on before you start working."

Working?

Though he didn't look at Zoey, his words hit her hard.

Did he see Daisy alerting on her and think that *she* needed the kind of care the dog offered?

Surely not.

It must have been a random, off-the-cuff remark that didn't mean anything. He must have meant that the hound would be working with Peyton as soon as they entered the federal building.

Frost vested Daisy, straightened his own tie, which he'd worn loose on the drive over, and then held out his free hand to Zoey as they headed for the courthouse. Zoey was ultra-aware of Frost's fingers clasping hers and was grateful for the comfort it offered, because suddenly, even though she was only here as an observer, she felt nervous.

Just before they reached the door, Frost pulled her to a stop and turned toward her, bending his head slightly.

"Do you mind if I say a little prayer before we go in?" he asked. "I've kind of made a habit of it."

"Not at all." And to her surprise, she really *didn't* mind. For the first time in a very long time, she wanted to pray. Somehow, her faith was returning. It had snuck up on her when she'd least expected it.

"Father," Frost whispered close enough to her ear that she could feel the warmth of his breath on her cheek, "today we lift up Peyton to you as she goes to court. Fill her with Your presence and strength, Lord, and wrap Your mantle of love around her and give her peace. Please allow Daisy to do her job and help Peyton remain calm. We pray in Christ's name. Amen."

"Amen," Zoey echoed, but her mind was still on Frost's words. She had been carrying around the burden of hate for so long that it had become a living part of her. She'd turned her back on God, had believed He had abandoned her after that horrible night.

Was it the other way around?

She had no more time to ponder those thoughts as they went through security and found the room where Peyton and her lawyers were waiting for them to arrive.

After introductions were made, Frost brought Daisy to Peyton's side and introduced her to the dog. Peyton was a pretty blonde who wore fake eyelashes that made her eyes look huge. She appeared as if she belonged on a college campus. Zoey could see why Frost had called her a young lady, even though she was only a few years younger than they were.

She turned her attention back to what Frost was doing. Without even so much as a verbal command, Daisy sat in between Peyton's legs and laid her muzzle on her knee.

Peyton smiled shakily and ran a hand across the dog's head.

"Daisy is here to support you, Peyton, and help you feel safe while on the stand," Frost explained. "While I know you have to pay close attention to what's going on while you're on the witness stand, you can keep your gaze on her whenever you need to stay calm. Just leave your hand on her head and pet her whenever you feel your anxiety rising. She will take her cues from you. If you need to focus somewhere other than the defense lawyer, look at Daisy. Interact with her. Take whatever time you need, even if that means you don't answer questions right away. Everyone in the courtroom has been briefed as to why Daisy is there, and they won't mind if you need to take an occasional breath. Are you ready to practice?"

Peyton's green eyes turned glassy, and she sniffled. One of her lawyers offered her a box of tissues, and she took one to blink back her tears and dab underneath her eyes in that way women had of trying to make sure their mascara wasn't running.

"I promised myself I wasn't going to cry," she said, tightening her jaw and blinking several times.

Zoey felt mad respect for Peyton. She didn't know if she'd have the kind of courage the young woman was showing. She wouldn't be able to project half her strength. She knew that for a fact because she'd lived through something similar and hadn't shown any strength at all. Instead, she'd wallowed in her misery and made one mistake after another.

"If you feel as if you're losing hold of your emotions or are panicking, just focus on Daisy," Frost said again. "And if she bumps your hand with her muzzle, that's a sign that you should take a moment and a few deep breaths. She senses your feelings and heart rate and will respond to them."

"You don't have to look at the defendant." One of the lawyers said. "Not until they ask you to point him out in the courtroom. In fact, it's better if you don't look at him, as he may try to make eye contact with you and get inside your head."

Peyton gave a wobbly nod and then turned her attention to Frost. "Thank you for letting me use Daisy today. I think she's really going to help me keep my nerves from getting the best of me."

"She will," Frost agreed. "It's her special gift, what she was born to do. I knew that even before I trained her for this."

Zoey thought about the times when she'd seemed to connect with Daisy, as if the dog could feel her emotions. Daisy had calmed her heart on more than one occasion. She prayed Daisy could do the same for Peyton.

Chapter Eight

Since the prosecution had finished up just before lunch and they'd called an hour-and-a-half break, Frost took Zoey out to eat. He could tell how moved Zoey had been by what she had seen so far that day, so he kept the conversation light and away from the trial.

When they returned to court, the prosecution lawyers were just setting up at their table in the courtroom. Peyton was sitting upright, staring straight ahead, her jaw taut and her shoulders tense.

The defense was not yet in the room. Frost suggested to Zoey that she find a seat wherever she was most comfortable, because he needed to be sitting up front at the table by Peyton, at least until her part of the trial was over.

He sat down in the chair on the right side of Peyton and placed Daisy to his left, so Peyton could reach out and touch the dog whenever she needed her. He was surprised that she wanted to be in the room at all before she was called, since she'd been given the option to wait outside the courtroom and be ushered in at the appropriate moment.

Peyton was a brave woman who Frost greatly admired.

And speaking of brave women—

Just as the defense entered the room, Frost glanced back to see how Zoey was faring. She was staring straight at

Dawson as he shuffled forward. A frown lined her face, and her gaze was narrowed; he wondered what she was thinking. Dawson was cuffed hand and foot but was wearing a regular gray suit and tie rather than an orange jumpsuit. Slouching as he walked, he surveyed the room with squinty eyes and a taut jaw, and Frost wondered if he may have made a mistake in bringing Zoey here today. Just being in the room with such a man was frightening. Even Frost felt the chill as Dawson was helped into his seat.

While he was excited for Zoey to see what Daisy could do in this unique situation, he also knew how sensitive and empathetic Zoey was, and he suddenly felt a little selfish for inviting her. He should have realized that watching Peyton stand up to the man who'd hurt her might be more than Zoey could emotionally handle.

Daisy would help, of course, but there was only one Daisy and two women who needed her right now.

But to his surprise, when Zoey realized he'd glanced back at her, she met his gaze straight on and nodded once, a quick jerk of her chin.

He got the message.

Get it done.

Frost turned his attention back to Peyton and offered her an encouraging smile, bending his head to whisper last-minute reminders about how to use Daisy when she took the stand. She was already stroking Daisy's head with her palm in a rhythmic pattern that matched her quick breaths. Her gaze was glassy with anxiety, but she had a determined set to her jaw.

They stood as the judge entered, and then the defense started their case. As Frost had suspected, they had almost nothing to present to the jury, and it wasn't long before they called Peyton to the stand.

Frost accompanied her to the witness stand and waited until she'd been sworn in and seated before situating Daisy in between her legs. Daisy immediately put her muzzle on Peyton's knee and nuzzled her hand, and Peyton pressed her palm onto the dog's head. Frost could see she was shaking, and he offered her an encouraging smile before returning to the prosecution's table.

The defense lawyer started peppering Peyton with question after question in an aggressive fashion, just as the prosecution had warned her they would do. They were doing everything they could to get her to break down, slip up or give up entirely.

It didn't take long for him to see just how courageous Peyton was. Whenever she prepared to answer one of the defense lawyer's questions, she paused, took a deep breath, and gave Daisy's floppy ears a scratch. Then she'd straighten her shoulders and answer loudly and thoroughly.

He could see the huge difference in Peyton's expression when the prosecution was allowed to cross-examine her. She was clearly more relaxed, though she still had her hand on Daisy, who continued to nudge her muzzle underneath Peyton's palm.

After Peyton's testimony was over, Jensen asked her the question for which they'd all been waiting.

"Peyton," Jensen asked with a hint of the drama Frost had seen on television crime shows, looking from Peyton to the jury and then back again, "Is the man who drew his gun on you, robbed you and viciously pistol-whipped you in this room right now?"

Peyton nodded.

"Please, point out the man to whom you're referring."

Peyton pointed directly at Dawson.

Jensen then told the judge he had no further questions. The judge asked the defense for their cross-examination, but they deferred.

No doubt about it, Peyton and the prosecution had prevailed, partially due to Daisy's help. Now it was just a matter of making closing arguments and allowing the jury to adjourn and discuss the case. Frost quickly stepped forward to take the dog, congratulating Peyton on her good effort and telling her how amazing she'd been.

As he turned to take Daisy out for some air, he looked for Zoey. She wasn't sitting where he'd last seen her—nor was she anywhere else in the courtroom.

She was gone.

Zoey had fled the courtroom the moment she was able to, feeling claustrophobic in the suddenly small room after Peyton had gone into detail about everything that had happened to her.

Zoey's pulse was pounding in her ears, indicating a coming migraine, and she suspected it was going to be a bad one. Whether from the headache or from what she'd just witnessed, she felt nauseated as Peyton's story echoed in her mind over and over again.

She couldn't get outside fast enough, seeking fresh, crisp air and the wide-open sky, even if it was shaded by the skyscrapers looming all around her. Frantically, she dug through her purse, searching for her migraine medicine to stave off the pain. If she didn't take it now, her headache would get ahead of her, and she might be suffering for days. She may already be too late.

Her phone buzzed with a text from Frost.

Hey. Where are you?

She'd nearly forgotten about Frost in her haste to bolt from the courthouse.

Out by your SUV. Sorry. Migraine. Needed fresh air.

He knew she suffered from chronic migraines, but today was about so much more than that. Was there any possibility that he would just let this one go and not question her about it?

Doubtful.

Frost was sensitive that way and would know something besides just her headache was wrong with her—not that running headlong out of the courtroom without letting him know where she was going had been a blatant clue.

Minutes later, she saw Frost exit the building with Daisy at his heel. Zoey waved and attempted to smile, but it turned out to be more of a grimace of pain.

Frost may or may not have noticed her pathetic attempt at a greeting, but Daisy definitely did.

Barooo!

With a half bark, half howl common to beagles, Daisy lunged, yanking the lead out of Frost's hands as she dashed to Zoey's side, where she bumped her leg with her muzzle, nearly knocking her off her feet in the process.

Zoey realized Daisy was just what she needed right now—offering her comfort, and she crouched down and wrapped her arms around the dog, burying her face in the soft fur of her neck.

Daisy responded by wiggling even closer and licking her chin, then howling adorably. This time Zoey's smile was for real. She'd never owned a dog, but now she wondered why she hadn't. Daisy was amazing in so many ways.

"Are you okay?" Frost asked as he approached, the concern in his voice obvious.

"Oh, yeah," she said, trying to sound as if she meant it. She didn't want to have to get into the truth with him. "Hit by a sudden migraine. Nothing new there."

"When I turned around after Peyton's testimony and you weren't there, I was concerned about you."

"I just needed some fresh air and didn't wait to let you know. Sorry if I worried you unnecessarily."

He didn't look convinced. He glanced at the dog and then back at her.

"Okay," he agreed hesitantly, but then shook his head. "No. It's not okay. Daisy is alerting on you, and it has nothing to do with a headache. I think this is all my fault, and I apologize, not that words will mean anything now."

"What?" she asked, confused. "Daisy is alerting on me?"

"I never should have brought you here today. I don't know why I ever thought that would be a good idea. I have a hard enough time watching these trials myself, and I know what a sensitive heart you have. It must have been especially painful for you to watch what happened today, to hear what Peyton went through."

That was true, but not for the reasons Frost imagined. As bad as Peyton's story was, that wasn't what had so moved Zoey. It was her own story, hidden deep within the depths of her heart, that was making her feel sick right now.

So, should she tell him the real reason Daisy was alerting on her or leave Frost in the dark?

"I've certainly never experienced anything like what I saw today," she admitted, leading him away from the real reason Daisy was alerting on her. "It isn't anything at all like the kind of courtroom drama you see on TV."

"That's for sure. I had my fists clenched nearly the entire time Peyton was on the stand."

"I agree with you. I was upset just watching poor Peyton getting peppered with questions."

"Peyton was amazing. She really held it together."

"I'll say. She was way more courageous than I could ever be in similar circumstances. And Daisy was incredible, too."

His gaze narrowed on her. He opened his mouth as if to speak but then closed it again. The silence between them was painful, and Zoey knew it was all on her. Staying silent about her truth was hurting their relationship, and the twins depended on that relationship to work so they could co-parent.

She knew Frost suspected more, but she still couldn't speak. She had a lot of praying to do before she'd be ready for that.

"Can you—would you mind swinging by the church before we go home? I know you're anxious to see the twins. I am, too. But I just need a moment with God."

He chuckled as he put Daisy in her kennel for the ride home. "You know you don't need to go to an actual church to talk to God. He's everywhere. Though, in fairness, I have to admit I did the very same thing a couple of weeks ago."

"It may seem silly, but I just need a moment of peace and quiet to center my thoughts, my heart and soul. As soon as I go home to the twins, that's not going to happen. It's twenty-four/seven utter chaos with those two."

"Sure. I get it."

"You can just drop me off. I can walk home from the church. You don't have to wait for me."

His gaze caught hers. Did he look worried? Disappointed? Probably. Because if he dropped her off, he wouldn't get to see the babies.

His mouth twisted into a wry smile. "In those heels? No way. I'll wait for you. Besides, I'd like to peek in on the twins, if that's okay with you."

So, it was just as she'd suspected—he wanted to spend time with the babies. She ignored her own little twinge of disappointment that he didn't want to wait with her for her sake and let her heart warm as they continued to lock gazes.

Thank you, Jesus, that Frost is Dante and Ari's father.

As if Frost knew she was praying, he said, "You know, I'm glad to hear you're returning to your faith. You really encouraged me with the strength of your love for God back when we used to date. I don't know what happened in college after we broke up, but I know how tough faith journeys can sometimes be."

Zoey cringed inwardly, knowing she must have had something to do with Frost's own difficulties.

All things work together for good, she reminded herself as Frost pulled into the church parking lot.

All things—even this.

Chapter Nine

On Sunday morning, Frost was pleased to see Zoey in church for the first time since she'd returned to Whispering Pines. He barely had a moment to speak to her, as she was warmly welcomed back by the community. She'd clearly been missed, and Frost enjoyed watching her being embraced by her faith community. And, of course, everyone was thrilled to meet the twins.

He knew firsthand what it felt like to have trauma draw a person away from their faith, as it had happened to him after his parents died in a car accident when he and his siblings had been teens. He had been angry with God for years. It had actually taken another heartbreak to turn him back to the Lord.

He still wasn't sure what was really going on with Zoey, but he became more convinced by the day that it hadn't been his proposal, or even the surprise pregnancy, that lay so heavily on her heart. It was something else. Something big.

On Monday, Frost hurried through his morning chores with the animals so that he could visit with Zoey and the kids in the afternoon. This was becoming an almost daily encounter. Either he would visit Zoey's mom's house or Zoey would bring the twins to the farm for some Daddy-babies time. Even at their young age, the kids loved the animals, which thrilled Frost. He saw so much of Zoey in the babies' personalities, so it was nice to see something of himself in them besides their physical characteristics of blond, curly hair and blue eyes.

The moment he stepped out of his truck in front of the Lanes' house, he could hear the sound of a baby wailing. He knew the twins well enough by now to know it was Ari's cry, and he hurried to the door. Dante was the whiner and usually only used his voice when he wanted something. Ari, on the other hand, chattered a lot but rarely fussed, so the sound of her crying in distress immediately worried him. When the door opened, he was met with an exhausted-looking Zoey holding an inconsolable Ari. She was screaming, stiffening her whole body indignantly as she yanked on Zoey's hair.

Frost stepped right into the fray, gently untangling Ari's tiny fingers from Zoey's hair and taking her into his arms, shifting her onto his shoulder.

"Shh," he said, gently patting Ari's back. "What's wrong, baby girl? Tell your daddy all about it."

"They both got immunization shots today in both legs. Dante has mostly been sleeping it off, but it's been tough on poor Ari. She's been fussy all afternoon, poor thing."

Frost kissed Ari's soft cheek, which was wet with tears. "I'm sorry you're feeling poorly, sweetheart. Do you want to dance with Daddy?"

He sang a quiet, rhythmic, low-voiced lullaby, which he accompanied with a gentle swaying motion. Within minutes, Ari had stopped wailing and was sucking on her fist, her eyes still wide open and blinking up at Frost in a way that made his heart turn over.

"You are such a show-off," Zoey accused, though she was smiling and looked relieved. "I've been walking her around for what feels like a lifetime, and then you come in and calm her down in no time at all."

"Maybe she just liked my song," he suggested, not able to suppress the grin that curled his lips.

"Yeah. Or your voice. Or the way the sound echoes through your chest. You know you melt all the ladies' hearts with that smooth tenor of yours. You always have. Where'd you learn the lullaby? I've never heard it before. Is it an old family favorite?"

Through the rumbling in his chest, he tried not to laugh; Ari's eyes were drifting closed, and he didn't want to disturb her.

"YouTube," he admitted in a whisper. "It's kind of embarrassing to admit, but I spent that first night after I learned I was a father looking up lullabies on the internet— that and spending a ton of time searching websites on everything I needed to know and get for a baby's first year. I didn't sleep at all, but I managed to fill a spiral notebook full of useful notes. I'm still referring to them quite often, as a matter of fact."

"That is so cute." Zoey covered her mouth to smother a giggle. "Maybe you ought to write your own book on baby care from a father's perspective. You'll be an expert before you know it, after all, especially with twins. And I can just imagine you crouched over your guitar trying to learn a whole new genre of music in one night. Did you stick with the classics or also learn some of the newer kids' TV theme songs? Some of those stick in your mind like earworms."

"Oh, sure. Go ahead and laugh. You had nine months

to prepare before the babies arrived, remember? I only had a day. However surprised you may have been at discovering you were pregnant, I was doubly so when you showed up with the twins already in tow."

He regretted the words the moment they left his mouth. The atmosphere in the room went from warm to icy in a split second.

"Zoey, I didn't mean—"

"No." She held up her hand, palm out. "No, you're right, and I deserve your censure. I know exactly what you mean. I pulled the rug out from underneath you."

"It was nothing more than a bad joke, spoken in haste and without thinking it through. Forgive me."

She nodded quickly, but he knew how bad he'd hurt her with his words.

"Ari's asleep, thanks to you," Zoey said, holding out her hands for the baby. "Do you want to put her down?"

His heart immediately balked. He knew if Zoey put her down, with Dante still sleeping, he'd have to leave, and he wasn't quite ready to do that yet.

"Can I just sit and rock her for a while?" he asked, not moving to hand Ari over to her. "It's nice just to hold her in my arms." And, while it was true that he was trying extra hard to stay in the moment and enjoy cuddling his babies every opportunity he had—they were growing and changing every day and he didn't want to miss a moment—if he was being completely honest with himself, staying around right now wasn't all about his daughter.

He wasn't prepared to leave yet because he hadn't spent any time with *Zoey* today, and as the days went on and they spent time together with the twins, he was starting to remember why they'd once been a happy couple. They had an unspoken connection that hadn't gone away with time or heartache. They understood each other in a way he'd never experienced with any other person. And while he was more than aware that the time had long passed by for them to ever again be a couple, he still found himself wanting to spend as much time with her as possible.

Zoey smiled, her gaze tender, and she gestured toward the rocker where he carefully seated himself so as not to wake Ari. The baby stirred, turning her head so her face was burrowed into his neck before sighing in her sleep. Her tiny lips turned into a pout that grabbed Frost's heart and squeezed it tight.

"Oh, no. No sad faces," Zoey said quietly, tucking Ari's blanket around her and pulling an armchair next to Frost so she could watch Ari sleep as well.

Ari didn't wake from whatever had startled her and caused her to stir; instead, she fell into a deep sleep, her jaw dropping and the cutest little snore emerging from her toothless mouth. Frost relaxed his shoulder and snuggled her tighter, unable to process the myriad emotions swirling through him.

"I hate it when she makes those little pouty faces in her sleep and looks as if she might break into tears," Zoey said. "Sometimes she'll smile or giggle, and I love it when that happens. I always wonder what she's dreaming about, and it stirs my heart every time."

"Yeah," he agreed, his chest tightening. "I never want her to have a reason to cry, awake or asleep. I suppose that's one of the most difficult parts about being a parent. It's up to us to do everything we can to shield them from the bad things in life. We want to protect them from everything. We don't ever want to see them hurt or have their hearts broken. But as much as we'd like to, we can't do that, can we?"

It hurt his heart just to think about all the things he *couldn't* do for his children. How he'd have to step back and watch them make their own mistakes and suffer their own sorrows. From the time they were born, they were moving away from their parents and toward the big, wide, scary world, and it hurt his heart just to think about it.

"That's where it's important to remember our most precious children are also God's children and are in the Lord's hands. He can take care of them far better than we are able to, anyway."

"That's true." Frost wondered where this strong woman had come from and how he'd been blessed to be connected to her in this way. His faith felt weak next to hers, and he closed his eyes for a moment, pulling strength from her.

"I love the way the twins have taken to you," she said, nodding at the contentedly sleeping Ari. "They knew you were their daddy from the very first time you held them in your arms."

He brushed a hand over Ari's baby-soft curls. "I have to admit I was worried at first—about being a father, I mean. But I'm feeling more and more comfortable in the role with every day that goes by. It's funny, but now I can't imagine my life without the twins."

They sat quietly for a few minutes, Frost softly humming a classic lullaby and thinking about how nice it was to be in his children's lives and what a blessing they were.

Zoey suddenly shifted in her seat, rubbing her palms

across her jeans in what Frost recognized as a nervous gesture.

"So—I-I have a favor to ask you," she stammered. "Feel free to say no, but…"

Zoey didn't know why she was so nervous asking Frost for a simple favor that would be no big deal if she was requesting it from any of her friends. But for some reason, it felt like a huge ask with Frost.

Part of the reason was that despite the time, distance and hurt feelings, Frost knew the deepest desires of her heart better than anyone else in this world. They weren't together as a couple now. She didn't know how to define their relationship. But he knew her well enough to understand how important her next words were.

She needed to use his dog.

"Ask away," Frost said, his silver-blue eyes filled with curiosity.

"You know my audition for the symphony is coming up at the end of this week."

"Uh-huh. Right. Friday afternoon."

"Yes. At 3:30," she said, her voice shaking as she said the time.

"You sound a little nervous, but you shouldn't be. You know you're going to rock your audition, just like you always do. They'll be begging you to come play for them and be happy to do it."

She scoffed. She wished she had even half the confidence Frost was showing her just now. He always had been supportive of her career dreams and goals.

"Actually, I *am* nervous," she admitted. "I feel insecure just thinking about it. I can't even imagine what my violin is going to sound like if I can't stop this quivering." She held up her hand to demonstrate.

"Let out all your nerves now, and then you'll be fine when it comes time to play. It's not as if this is the first audition you've ever had. You had to audition in high school and to get into college."

"That's true, but this audition is the most important one I've ever had. It's not a matter of what orchestra I'll get into in school. This will change my whole life one way or another—where I will end up living, what kind of music I'll be playing."

"True."

"So, my point is that basically I'm incredibly uneasy and want to be concentrating on my audition instead of driving. So, I'd prefer to have someone else take me to Denver, and that way my mind will be free to focus."

"Are you asking me for a ride?" he said, his voice rising in what sounded like excitement. If she wasn't already so full of anxiety, she would have laughed at the expression on his face.

"Well, I mean, only if you want to."

"Oh, I want to," he assured her quickly. "I mean, I'd be honored. I thought you were going to ask me to take care of the twins, but I will absolutely drive you to your audition, and I'll pray for you the whole time you're there."

"I appreciate that more than you know, but I actually have a hidden motive for asking you specifically to drive me downtown."

He raised his eyebrows. "Okay." He drew out the word, sounding confused.

"Your dog," she blurted out quickly, not knowing why

she was having so much trouble making such a simple request. "Daisy. Can we bring her with us on the ride?"

If he was surprised by the request, he didn't show it. His eyes shined as he smiled widely. "I think that's a great idea. Daisy is a pro at helping you keep your nerves in check."

"That's what I was thinking. After watching her work with Peyton, I thought maybe she could do the same for me."

"No question about it," he assured her.

She paused and pursed her lips. "I'll be wearing all black again, though. That's probably the worst color I could choose for rubbing up against a shedding dog."

"No worries. Have lint roller, will travel. I'm your guy."

Zoey's breath caught in her throat as their eyes met and held. She knew he was teasing her, but his words struck her right in the solar plexus and then radiated up to her heart.

He *had* been her guy. He'd always been the man for her, and there had been no one since him.

What would her future look like, and what kind of messed-up version of life was she heading toward?

The twins would grow up—far too fast for her liking—and eventually go to school.

Frost would always be a part of her life—probably a big part. They would co-parent the twins as best they could. She thought they'd probably be amicable toward each other. But Frost's life would go on as well. He would no doubt marry and have a family of his own.

And suddenly she felt very, very alone.

When she'd first come back to Whispering Pines, she'd felt a lot different than she did now. She hadn't known how Frost was going to feel about any of this—her or the children. They still had a long way to go, but they'd made a lot of progress in their relationship.

Dante yelled from his play yard in the bedroom, and Zoey smiled. "He always wakes up happy, hungry and loud," she said with a laugh.

Frost grinned and patted his trim stomach. "Now *that* is definitely my son."

"He's already eating some solid foods. Formula isn't enough for him," she said. "Mouth open, insert food."

"I get that," Frost said with a wink. "He is developing into a big, strong boy. Not that I want him to grow up too fast, but I have to admit I can't wait to toss a football with him."

Zoey raised her eyebrows. "Aren't you forgetting someone?"

He chuckled. "Of course not. Ari will be out there beating us both with her accuracy and strong throwing arm."

"You'd better believe it."

She'd known he would be the dad out playing football with *both* his kids. She could practically picture him now, chasing after Ari, who would have the football and be zigzagging around the yard. Frost would pick her up and swing her around in lieu of tackling her.

Yes, he was going to be a phenomenal father to the twins.

"And don't forget you'll be out there, too," he reminded her. "I seem to remember you were pretty handy with the football yourself, back in the day."

She remembered it, too—those times back in high school when they'd toss a football back and forth at the park. It had been so simple back then, and so romantic.

She'd catch the ball and run, and he'd grab her around the waist and swing her around before kissing her until she was dizzy.

She could tell by the look on his face that he was remembering the same thing.

They weren't a couple anymore, but maybe they could build some type of family together, one with its own set of guidelines. Only time would tell.

Chapter Ten

Frost rose extra early on Friday morning to make sure he had plenty of time to clean up after he was finished with his chores. He wanted to look his best today, despite the fact that he wasn't the one going in for the audition. So he dressed in his best suit and tie. He wanted to let Zoey know he was firmly standing behind her and had her back.

His reasoning was that Zoey would be in her best outfit, so he would be, too, even if he was only going to wait in the SUV and pray while she went in and played her best audition.

When he approached Zoey's mom's house, he let Daisy out of the front passenger seat of the SUV, where she'd be riding along with Zoey rather than her usual place in the kennel in back.

He was just reaching out to knock on the door when Zoey's mom opened it, her index finger over her lips to indicate he should speak quietly because one or both babies were asleep.

"Hello, Daisy," she said in a low voice, greeting the dog by rubbing her floppy ears. She stood and looked at Frost. "Zoey will be right out," she whispered. "She's just putting the finishing touches on her makeup."

He smiled and nodded, slipping his hands into the pockets of his slacks, and rocking back on his heels. In his mind, Zoey didn't even need makeup to look stunning, but he knew making herself up would give her extra confidence. Lizzie went to check on Zoey's progress, and Frost glanced around the living room as he waited.

He noticed a stack of brochures on the end table closest to the front door and wandered over to see what they were, Daisy staying right at his heel.

Real estate brochures.

Local houses for sale in Whispering Pines.

His heart leapt with joy.

Did this mean she might be considering settling down permanently here in town?

She hadn't mentioned house hunting at all, but the thought that she might stay around close enough for him to see her and the twins every day made his adrenaline kick into high gear.

Having his babies around him meant a lot, as Zoey well knew. And he had to admit having Zoey close by wasn't such a bad idea, either.

He was so deep in thought, he didn't even realize Zoey was behind him until she touched his shoulder. He didn't know why, but he whirled around, feeling as if he'd been caught with his hand in the cookie jar. Maybe it was because she hadn't said anything to him about settling down in Whispering Pines. Perhaps she didn't yet want him to know of her plans until she'd made a solid decision to stay.

Or to go.

His emotions were zipping all over the place, but naturally, Daisy had already abandoned him for her. Even though the whole reason he'd brought Daisy today was for

Zoey's sake, Frost still felt a little bit betrayed and abandoned that his dog would pick Zoey's crisis over his own.

He mentally shook himself out of it, reminding himself of the real reason why he'd outfitted himself up in this monkey suit. Daisy was present for Zoey, and so was he.

Zoey was dressed in the same pretty black outfit she'd worn the day of court, but for some reason she looked much stiffer and more formal today, which he suspected was more from her anxiety than it was the clothing.

Rather than speaking, he swept his hand toward the door, and she smiled weakly and gave him a shaky nod. "Mom will take the twins to your Gramps's and Nan's house later today before she goes off to Golden with her friends to get some shopping done. You sure they'll be okay with both babies?"

"Don't ask them that out loud. I learned the hard way. I got a lecture on lineage that sounded as if it was something out of the Bible. You know—so-and-so begat so-and-so, and on and on. And apparently, they single-handedly cared for all the children from infancy on up, which isn't exactly accurate, but it is true that they've each had lots of childcare experience over the years."

Zoey chuckled. "I guess we can depend on them, then."

Frost nodded. "Count on it. I totally trust them."

Outside, Zoey opened the rear door and carefully set her violin on the back seat while Frost opened the front passenger-side door. "Go ahead and hop in. I thought Daisy could ride in the front with you today rather than in her kennel in the back."

"*Such* a good idea," she agreed. "That way I can pet her the whole way down." Strain was evident in her voice as her mind had seemingly returned to the reason they were taking Daisy with them today—the audition still ahead of her, her dream, the one that would literally change her life.

"And don't worry. I've got you covered—or rather, un-covered. Recovered? I brought three lint rollers with me just in case Daisy sheds on your black clothing."

He got a small chuckle out of her, for which he was thankful. Anything he could do to keep her mind off her anxiety was a good thing.

"How's your head feeling today?" he asked, knowing of Zoey's chronic migraines.

"I've already taken medicine in anticipation of the day. Hopefully that will stave off the headache I know is about to come. You know how stress always gets to me."

"Yeah," he agreed, sending up a silent prayer that today would be headache-free for her. She struggled so much with her migraines, and she was already so nervous.

Lord, give her a clear, pain-free mind today.

Instead of talking to Frost as they drove down to Denver, the few comments she did make were to Daisy, who was leaning between Zoey's knees with her muzzle resting on Zoey's leg.

Otherwise, Zoey was silent and meditative, perhaps going over her music as she stared out the window at the passing forest scenery.

Frost took his cues from Zoey and Daisy and kept his thoughts to himself. Whenever he got nervous, his tendency was to yammer on and talk too much, but he knew Zoey was the exact opposite and clammed up, becoming introspective.

When they reached the Denver Center for the Performing Arts's multilevel parking garage, Frost wound his way around in circles until he found a parking space next to the elevator. It would take them to the ground level across from the Boettcher Concert Hall where the auditions were being held and where the symphony usually played.

Frost immediately sprang from the driver's side and hustled over to open the door for Zoey. He called Daisy down from the SUV and out of the way to make it easier for Zoey to exit the vehicle. But she just sat there, her fists clenched together in her lap, staring forward and breathing in heavy gasps.

"Zoey?" Frost asked, gently touching her arm, but she didn't immediately respond. She didn't even appear to be aware of his presence.

He'd accompanied her to several auditions over the years, but he'd never before seen her appear nervous and hesitant. She was usually so confident, cheerful and clear-headed.

"Right," she finally said, unfolding herself from the seat and brushing herself off. "It's only my entire future I'm facing here today. No big deal."

Wordlessly, Frost handed her a lint roller so she could un-Daisify herself of dog hair. He wanted to point out that while he knew that playing with the Colorado Symphony had always been her dream, with her talent on the violin, it was only one of many exciting career paths she could take. She could play for a theatre—the Buell, even, which often hosted touring Broadway shows. She could play for movie soundtracks or even for a band. Or she could audition for another state's symphony altogether.

Not that he wanted most of those things to happen—not anything that would take Zoey and the babies away from him.

But no. There was nothing to worry about. He had

every confidence she would rock her audition this afternoon and be invited to play with the symphony.

He held out his arms to Zoey and she slipped into his embrace, tightening her arms around him and squeezing the breath from his lungs. He inhaled the light strawberry scent of her shampoo and then brushed a kiss on her forehead.

"I believe in you. Go get them, honey."

Horrible.
Terrible.
Agonizing.
Humiliating.

Zoey's audition couldn't have been worse if she'd tried. She blinked back the tears stinging and burning in the back of her eyes as she returned her violin to her case as fast as she could manage. Thankfully, that was second nature to her and wasn't anything she needed to concentrate on to do.

And then, with equal promptness and as much dignity as she could muster, she held her head up and pulled her shoulders back as she made for the exit.

"Thank you for coming in today for the audition. If necessary, callbacks will be by the end of next week," one of the directors said. "We'll be making our decision by the fifteenth of the month."

He handed her a sheet of paper with all the pertinent dates and information—details she already knew she wasn't going to need. They weren't going to select her.

Whatever made her think she could play at the skill level required for the symphony? She hadn't been able to perfectly play her piece even though she'd practiced and practiced to do her best. But she'd just been fooling herself all along.

As she exited the building, she immediately noticed that the mild morning weather had quickly turned into a snowy afternoon. There was already two inches of fluffy flakes on the ground and, looking at the pure white skies, it didn't look as if it would be stopping anytime soon. The roads would be snow-packed and iced over before they knew it.

Only in Colorado could a woman get a sunburn in the morning and frostbite in the evening of the same day. And to make it worse, barometer fluctuations pressed and pulsed on her already throbbing headache. Stress and weather were a devastating combination for someone who suffered with chronic migraines. So much for the medicine she'd taken earlier for cutting her headache off at the pass. It wasn't anywhere close to enough. She closed her eyes for a moment against the stabbing pain.

Frost met her with an excited, anticipatory grin and wrapped his wool-lined jean jacket around her, since she wasn't wearing a coat. He must have tossed it in the back seat before they'd left, since he was wearing a suit jacket. The jean jacket smelled uniquely of Frost, a combination of the scent of pine trees, horses, and something indelible that was uniquely Frost, and somehow, deeply inhaling it calmed her down. As if in greeting, Daisy barked merrily as she approached, but then just as quickly she tipped her head to the side as she looked at Zoey with her huge, compassionate brown eyes. Her bark then turned into a howl, a whine of concern.

Apparently not seeing her pained expression—or misreading the hot tears she could no longer keep from rolling down her cheeks—Frost picked her up and swung her around with a happy whoop.

"Frost, no," she protested, pushing him away with her palms at the same time Daisy inched between them, leaning toward Zoey and nudging her leg.

He frowned, his blond eyebrows forming a low V over his silver-blue eyes. His gaze changed from exultant to concerned in an instant. "Honey, are you okay? What are the tears all about? What happened?"

She cringed at his casual use of his old pet name for her, making her feel even worse. He probably didn't even realize—didn't remember.

"It's over," she whispered raggedly, so low she didn't think he could hear her. She shook her head and scoffed.

"What do you mean?" His voice was soft and tender, but also filled with disbelief, and that was the part that really hurt, grabbing her gut and twisting it in a knot.

Frost believed in her far more than what she deserved. He always had, ever since they'd first started dating back in high school. He'd always had her back. And that was exactly why having to explain what had happened in the concert hall was sheer, razor-sharp agony to her heart.

It wasn't her ego so much that was bothering her. Rather, it was her life's dream being shredded right in front of her eyes.

And now Frost was a witness to it all.

She couldn't possibly have felt more humiliated than she did at that moment.

She set her violin in the back seat of the SUV, as careful with the instrument as always out of habit. Then she crouched next to Daisy and buried her face in the pup's neck, scratching her floppy ears and accepting the uncon-ditional love only a dog could give.

She was thankful Frost gave her the space she needed with Daisy without pushing her, offering as much time as she needed to pull herself together.

After a while, she stood and brushed the tears from her eyes with her palms, knowing her makeup must look a complete mess.

But what did that matter now?

"I appreciate that you were so sweet to take the time out of your busy day to bring me down here, but—"

She paused and swallowed hard, unable to finish her sentence. Frost called Daisy onto the passenger seat and positioned her so it would be easier for Zoey to interact with her.

Then Frost took both of Zoey's hands in his and dipped his head, capturing her gaze and locking it with his.

"Zoey, your hands are freezing." He ran his thumb across her knuckles and warmth flooded through her, but the chill she felt wasn't due to the change in weather so much as a natural physical response to the grief and dis-appointment she was feeling.

"What's going on?" he asked gently. "How can I help?"

That was *so* Frost, and her heart thawed for a short mo-ment before plunging back down into her stomach again.

"I blew it." Finally, she said the words aloud. She waited for a sense of relief that didn't come.

"What do you mean?"

Great. He wanted her to elaborate when all she wanted was to curl up in a ball and nurse her hurts.

"I mean I screwed it up. Ruined my audition single-handedly. I missed a run, played a couple of blatantly wrong notes, and flubbed one of my scales. I actually had to stop and apologize before jumping back into the piece." That last part had been the worst since she was perfectly aware a true professional would just have kept on playing the music and not stopped for an error, which a general audience may or may not have picked up on, but the audition judges would definitely have noticed.

"Oh, wow," Frost murmured. "Okay, well, that doesn't necessarily mean they won't ask you to join them. You won't know until they phone for callbacks, right?"

She shook her head almost violently. "I know there will be no callback for me. Please don't torture me with this."

Frost was silent for a long time. Zoey removed her hands from his grasp and once again turned her attention to Daisy.

"You're probably happy about this turn of events because now I'll have to stay in Whispering Pines," she accused in a sharp voice, knowing even as she said the words how unfair she was being to him. She'd jumped right past the denial stage of grief in the time it had taken her to pack up her violin and walk back to Frost's car.

Now she was just plain angry.

Angry at herself, not at Frost, but he was here and therefore receiving the brunt of her anger.

She knew she'd hurt his feelings with her blunt words, and they didn't speak again until they were well out of Denver and had crossed into the mountains.

"I'm sorry," she said at last. "I shouldn't have said what I did. I'm upset, but not at you, and I shouldn't have taken it out on you. I know that for you, where I end up living has everything to do with your being able to see your children on a regular basis. But for me, this was—"

"You think I don't understand how you're feeling right now?" His voice was tight with strain. "Well, I do. Maybe not exactly, but still. I had plans that didn't work out too, you know. Right before I found out I was the father of twins. I intended to finally go to college and get my degree so I could teach music at the middle and elementary schools. I even had my application ready to go. But I had to abandon those plans when you showed up with Dante and Ari."

"I didn't know. I'm sorry you think I ruined everything for you."

"That's not my point. You didn't ruin everything for me. I am every bit as responsible for the conception of the twins as you are. More, even, because I encouraged you to ignore your faith for me."

"I rationalized it in my mind, as well. Despite everything, that night was special. I wouldn't have done anything I didn't want to do...and we got the beautiful twins out of it." She sniffed, still not completely in control of her emotions.

And now to find out Frost believed he'd also had to give up on his dreams. She didn't understand how things could have gone so wrong.

It's too much, God. You promised us you wouldn't give us more than we could bear, but it's too much.

"I know you probably don't want to hear this right now, but even if you really did blow your audition, and I'm not thoroughly convinced you did, there are so many more things you can do with your aptitude with the violin, places that would be blessed to have a violinist with your talent join them. Your opportunities are limitless."

"Even if those opportunities would take me away from

Colorado?" she couldn't help asking. Again, with the jabs. Why was she doing this? Just because she was hurting inside didn't mean Frost had to hurt, too. He'd been nothing but supportive of her and she was being downright mean to him.

She slid him a glance fast enough to see his Adam's apple bob as he blinked and swallowed hard.

"Even then," he finally answered. "I want you to be happy, Zoey. Of course, I hope you'll search for opportunities around here, but I can't force you to make decisions based on what is best for me. If your dreams end up leading you elsewhere, we'll deal with that when it happens."

He took a deep, audible breath and continued.

"I don't know what God has planned for us, but we have to keep believing He is leading us both, and our children, toward our best lives."

Best lives?

She wrapped her arms around herself and shivered, and not because of the cold.

She'd just flubbed up her only chance at her best life. Anything else would be second rate, wouldn't it?

She didn't even know what a second choice could be anymore.

Was there another *best life* out there she hadn't yet discovered?

Chapter Eleven

Frost turned on the SUV's four-wheel drive mechanism so he had more traction as he slowly made his way up the curvy mountain road. He'd been driving this route from the time he was fifteen and had years of experience on the winding Rocky Mountains roadways, but he still took his time. The snow was falling in big, white snowflakes now and sticking to the road under his tires. The wind had also picked up, creating almost whiteout conditions. He couldn't see but a few feet in front of him, and there was always the possibility of hitting a patch of black ice and completely losing control of the vehicle, a threat for even the most cautious of drivers.

Zoey rhythmically stroked Daisy's ears and neck, which was better than what he was doing, with both of his hands clamped white-knuckled to the steering wheel. He'd bumped up the heat to where he was nearly uncomfortably warm, yet Zoey was still trembling, even though she still had Frost's jacket wrapped around her shoulders, dwarfing her smaller stature. He was glad she'd thought to bring Daisy along. The dog was making all the difference in the world in keeping her calm, just as she'd been trained to do.

He was glad for that, at least. What a miserable day this

had turned out to be—on all fronts. The only thing that *didn't* seem to be wrong was Daisy's sensitivity.

By the time they reached the turnoff for Whispering Pines, there was at least eight inches of snow on the ground, and the weather app on Zoey's phone indicated it wasn't going to slow down anytime soon. Predictions were always questionable in a mountain town, but blizzard conditions and at least two feet of snow were slated for their area. It wasn't often that they had a storm of this magnitude, even in the mountains, but it had happened more than once, and at the rate the snow was falling today, Frost didn't doubt they were in for a major blast.

His biggest worry was that they had to go to the farm to pick up the twins before he could drop Zoey off at her mom's house. But he suspected once they reached the farm it was going to be difficult to go anywhere else, even simply back to town. He doubted Sharpe or any of his brothers-in-law would have had time to run the tractor and dig out the road yet. Plus, it didn't really make sense to do much before the snow stopped falling.

He was trying to figure out how to ask Zoey what she wanted to do about the tricky situation when her cell phone rang.

It was her mother, and they spoke for a few minutes before she hung up, her brows lowered, and her expression concerned.

"Mom couldn't make it up the pass in her car," Zoey said, absently reaching for Daisy and scratching her ears. "She had to turn around and go back to town."

"Is everything good?"

"Yes. She's safe. She's checked in at a local hotel until the storm blows over."

"That's a smart idea. I'm glad we won't have to be anxious about her driving up those slick mountain roads in this horrible weather. But given that your mom will be away, I'm also a little concerned about you and the twins being alone at your mom's house. You know how often the power goes out during storms like these."

"True enough. We've got LED lanterns and blankets, but I'll admit I don't like the idea of being alone with the babies during a power outage. What do you suggest?"

"The twins are already over at our ranch house with Gramps and Nan, so I think we should stay there. I need to take care of all the animals, too, but I'm even more concerned about the kids and would feel better if I was with them. And you," he added, making it sound almost like an afterthought, though it wasn't. "We have a generator, if it comes to that. We also have a nice, toasty woodstove that heats our house well, and a big hearth, too. We'll all be comfortable and safe. I even have cribs for the babies now."

And a swing, and a bouncer, and dozens of toys and books, but he wasn't going to mention those just yet. He *may* have gone overboard the first time he'd gone shopping for the twins.

"What do you think?" he asked, trying to tamper his enthusiasm at the prospect and sound as serious as he should be.

His stomach tightened into knots as he waited for her answer.

"This weather *is* crazy," she agreed. "And as I said, I'd rather not get caught alone with the babies in a blackout. Having you and Gramps and Nan around would be welcome."

"Good. Between the two of them, Gramps and Nan may seem like a real handful sometimes, but they're great with the twins. After helping raise me and my siblings, Gramps has had plenty of practice with babies. And Nan is a natural great-grandmother."

Zoey chuckled. "They are quite the pair. I crack up every time I'm with them. And I appreciate them watching the twins today so you could drive me down to Denver, but honestly, I'm sure they've had more than enough baby duty for one day. The twins are a lot."

"They were the ones who volunteered to keep them, but I'm sure you're right. They must be exhausted, between Dante's energy and Ari's constant babbling."

Frost's shoulders relaxed and he breathed out. He hadn't realized how much her answer meant to him until she spoke. He felt much better knowing he could take care of Zoey and the twins during the blizzard. It was the least he could do, and it made him feel more like a father. And also—well, he didn't know where he was with Zoey, so maybe it was better not to finish that thought.

In a way, he was grateful for the storm, because it had apparently taken Zoey's mind off the audition and turned it onto taking care of the twins. He knew this wasn't the end of the conversation about what was going to happen next, especially if she was right about not getting into the symphony, but it was good for her to distance herself from it a little bit before she talked about it again.

When they reached the farm, he parked the SUV directly in front of the ranch house steps and hurried around to open the door for Zoey. He held her hand, their fingers linked, as the two of them traversed the thick snow. Daisy was having a blast hopping and rolling around through the mounds of soft, wet snow.

Zoey's teeth chattered and she shivered despite Frost's heavy coat still wrapped around her shoulders. "Heels are definitely not the right choice of footwear for this weather."

Frost had completely forgotten she'd been wearing strappy sandals rather than sensible boots, and he immediately scooped her into his arms.

"Frost, no," she complained, though she looped her arms tightly around his neck and tucked herself closer to his chest, her cheek against his shoulder.

His face grew warm despite the chill in the air. "I can't believe I let you walk through the snow in heels. As humiliating as this feels right now, this is going to be one of those stories that gets passed around the bonfire until our grandchildren have heard about it. Grandpa making Grandma walk through the snow in heels." He grinned lopsidedly. "Anyway, I'll start a big fire in the hearth as soon as we get inside so you can warm up your feet."

Grandpa and Grandma. Why was it so easy for him to picture? Impossible. They wouldn't be together. Not like he'd once believed they would be.

When they reached the front door, Frost shifted so Zoey could knock rather than ring the doorbell, in case the twins were sleeping.

"Oh, my," Nan exclaimed when she opened the door and saw Frost with Zoey in his arms. "Are you okay? What happened?"

"I accidentally let Zoey walk through the snow in high heels," he explained, his face warming even more under

Nan's sharp perusal, especially when she frowned and tilted her head up at him.

"You *let* her?" Nan said, her voice crackled with age.

"You *let* me?" Zoey asked simultaneously.

"Well, I… I…" he stammered, gently lowering Zoey to the ground, keeping his arm snugly around her waist until he was sure she had her bearings.

Where was Gramps when Frost needed him? He needed some male backup here before his mouth got him into real trouble with the ladies. "I was just trying to help her. Her feet were going to freeze off," he muttered under his breath.

Zoey and Nan both chuckled at his obvious discomfort.

"Where are the babies?" Zoey asked as she shucked off Frost's coat and returned it to him. He hung it on the coatrack along with his cowboy hat and turned back to hear Nan's answer.

"Sound asleep in their cribs. Frost, you ought to see it. Your Gramps has a real talent with singing babies to sleep. Is that where you got your voice, then?"

"No question about that. His tenor beats mine by a mile. I'm just grateful I'm related to him and that he passed his musical genes on to me."

"You're being humble when you don't need to be," came Gramps's scratchy voice from the hallway. "You have a natural talent, son, one that can't be taught. More than I ever did, though the babies do seem to like my voice."

Now he finally joined them, long after Frost had opened his mouth and inserted both feet.

"Let me get you some warm socks for your cold feet," Nan said to Zoey. "I just took a load of Frost's clothes out of the dryer. They'll likely be rather large for you, though. But they should still do the trick."

"Nan does your laundry for you?" Zoey taunted, a whisper of a smile playing on her mouth.

Frost felt his cheeks warm even more under her teasing scrutiny.

"No," he said with a petulant shrug. "Not always. I usually live alone at the ranch house since everyone else went and got married and moved away into their own households. I've been doing my own laundry for years. Sometimes I even washed my own clothes in high school."

He wasn't about to admit that lately he didn't have to do his own laundry, housework or even cooking, not while Nan was living in the house as they waited for the new solid oak flooring to be completed in their own home. Nan had told him she didn't like to be bored and enjoyed taking care of people, but now it was all backfiring on him.

And how fair was that? It would have been rude of him not to let Nan do as she liked, right? And it wasn't as if he could have stopped her even if he'd wanted to.

"I'm going to go check on the animals," he said, deciding in this case discretion was the better part of valor.

He felt much more comfortable in the stable with Daisy at his heel than he had inside the house. At least he could breathe easily out here. Animals didn't judge or tease, even though he knew it had all been done in good fun. Nan and Zoey didn't mean anything by their words, but he was easily embarrassed, and admitting to Zoey that Nan had been doing his laundry had him blushing to the roots of his hair. Unfortunately, because he was blond and had a fair complexion, he felt sure everyone had noticed the way his face flushed. He'd probably looked like a ripe tomato in there. The snowy weather was just what he needed to cool off.

Despite the weather outside, the barn was nice and cozy. Whenever it stormed, Frost always made sure the doors and windows were latched secure against the snow and wind.

He moved from stall to stall, pitching alfalfa hay into each manger and making sure the water troughs were filled and not covered with ice. He would keep most of the animals in the barn until the storm blew over, and then he would let them all out to pasture again once the worst of it was past.

Though stabled in the barn for now, his horses enjoyed and thrived in the cooler weather, and they always had refuge if they wanted it. Frost had built a sturdy lean-to for them to shelter under if need be.

Frost checked on the rest of the animals, as well—some of which were inside the barn like the pigs and the donkeys. Others, like the goats and llamas with their thick winter coats, did fine outside with minimal housing even in the worst of the cold.

With all the animals fed and cared for, it was well past time for Frost to return to the house. He'd lingered a lot longer than he'd originally intended, and he had plenty of chores to do inside, as well, especially in preparation for a blackout. He'd already chopped plenty of wood for the woodstove and fireplace, so it was just a matter of hauling some inside to the mudroom for easier access and then stoking up the fires, which would be pleasant whether the power went off or not.

"Daddy's back," he announced when he walked in from the mudroom with his arms loaded with firewood. Both twins were now wide awake and watched him with interest as he dumped an armful of wood by the hearth.

"It's about time," Zoey said, bouncing Dante in her arms to keep him from fussing. "I was beginning to think you'd decided to bed down with the animals in the barn and let us all freeze to death in here."

He narrowed his gaze on her. "Don't think I wasn't tempted. The animals don't pick on me."

She pursed her lips, but a giggle escaped, nonetheless.

It was the best sound he'd heard all day. At least she didn't appear to be mulling over her audition anymore.

He gave Dante a raspberry on his tummy that made the baby boy squeal with delight, flinging his arms and legs so wildly that Zoey was having trouble controlling the baby and keeping him firmly in her grasp.

"Whoops. Sorry," Frost said with a laugh.

Zoey rolled her eyes and then grabbed Dante's chubby fist. "Punch him in the nose," she said, helping Dante bat at Frost.

"Oh, you got me, big man," Frost said, stepping backward with a lunge and a twist, sending Dante into a fit of giggles.

"Where's my baby girl?" he asked.

"In the kitchen sitting on Gramps's lap while Nan cooks us up a delicious batch of chili. Can't you smell it?"

"Mmm. My favorite," he said. He wanted to grab one of the babies and have some cuddle time, but he still needed to move more of the wood inside close to the hearth and woodstove, just in case. It sounded as if he'd have to fight for the babies' attention in any case—there was lots of love to go around in this household.

He crouched down and prepared the wood for the

woodstove, then moved over and dropped to his knees in front of the hearth, filling it with firewood and kindling. He would wait on both the woodstove and the fireplace, but he intended to light the hearth soon and was looking forward to the evening, power or no power. Firelight always had a calming effect on Frost, whether it was in the hearth or at the bonfire, and he hoped it would be the same for Zoey after the day she'd had.

She seemed to have moved past her melancholy and was enjoying her time with ever-active Dante. She was holding him in a standing position in her lap and he was pumping his chubby legs, working out his muscles.

"How long until he's crawling?" Frost asked, leaning back and pressing his palms to his knees as he finished building up the hearth.

"It'll be a while yet, but I expect he'll be an early crawler, as strong as he is. He has a lot of muscular dexterity. According to the charts, it's supposed to be somewhere between six and nine months, I think."

"And Ari?"

Zoey chuckled. "She's our little babbler. She loves to make eye contact and smile, and she makes long strings of sounds as if she's having a whole conversation."

"Her very first word was Gramps," said Gramps, bringing Ari into the living room and placing her in a bouncy chair before settling into an armchair with a contented groan.

"How do you figure that?" Frost asked. "That's a hard word for a toddler, much less a little baby."

"*Ga* was her first syllable."

"And…that makes her first word *Gramps* how?" Frost snorted.

"*Ga. Gramps.* Simple, clear and easy. I'm going to take it for the win, and no one is going to convince me otherwise."

"You wish, old man," Nan said, entering the room with a frilly apron tied about her waist and waving a black silicone ladle like a weapon. "She said *Nan* first. Absolutely no doubt about it. *Na-na-na-na-na.* Seems to me I'm winning this here race."

Gramps scoffed under his breath and crossed his arms.

"As much as I'd love to hear her saying *ma-ma*, that syllable is yet to come," Zoey admitted with a sigh. She looked at Frost and a slow grin emerged. "But I've heard her say *da-da* once in a while."

"Really?" Frost's heart suddenly felt as if it was going to burst out of his chest.

"You just need to catch her when she's saying *da-da* and then encourage her to connect that sound to you. Anytime she says *da-da*, repeat it and point to yourself."

"Kind of like training Daisy," he said, thoughtfully running a palm over the scruff on his jaw.

"No, *not* like training a dog. Seriously, Frost," Zoey said, huffing indignantly. "I can't believe you just said that. Training your babies like your dogs. Really."

He grinned and shrugged, happy to get a rise out of her.

"Chili's finished," Nan said brightly. "Come and get it."

"I'll get yours for you, since you have the baby," Frost offered to Zoey. "You stay put."

"I'm going to have to set him down to eat," she countered, straightening her shoulders. "But thank you anyway."

Zoey put Dante on his back on a play pad on the floor,

where he could bat at the toys dangling over him. "He'll stay amused long enough for me to eat."

The adults had just reached the kitchen when the lights flashed, flickered, and then went out, leaving them all in the moonless pitch darkness only mountain living could give.

"Frost?" Zoey called, sounding a little off-kilter.

He reached toward the sound of her voice, gently waving his arm until his hand brushed her arm. "Right here, honey. I'm right here."

Zoey immediately thought of the twins. She should have taken up Frost's offer to get her chili for her and stayed with them, although she wasn't sure what she would have been able to do when she couldn't see her hand in front of her face. She knew Frost kept an LED lantern somewhere in the family room but wasn't sure if she'd be able to find it in the dark.

As suddenly as the darkness had encompassed them, a bright light flickered on, causing Zoey to hold a hand over her eyes against the glare.

It was Nan, wearing a headlamp that looked to Zoey like something a coal miner would wear on his helmet. Despite the circumstances, or maybe because of them, it was all Zoey could do not to break into titters of nervous laughter at the incongruous sight.

"I've got this," Nan said as she headed out to check on the twins.

Gramps flipped on an LED lantern, flooding the entire kitchen with light. Zoey remembered growing up in the days of low-glowing, bad-smelling kerosene lanterns. The LED was much brighter and happily didn't carry a scent. Still worried about the babies, Zoey followed Nan into the family room, but the twins had evidently not been as frightened by the sudden darkness as she'd expected them to be. Ari was looking around curiously and calmly sucking her fist. Dante had managed to grab a dangling stuffed sheep from the toy above his head and was repeating, "Ba-ba-ba-ba-ba." That was little Dante, precious boy that he was. She suspected all his animal words were going to be the sounds they made instead of the proper names of the animals. *Baa-baa* for lamb and *woo-woo* for dog, since his first encounter with a canine had been a beagle.

"Go ahead and grab your bowl of chili," Nan told her. "I'll stay here with the twins until everyone else is settled."

Gramps had evidently taken over the kitchen, having moved the stockpot of chili to the top of the woodstove for warmth. He was serving up bowls of the hearty meal with a side of fresh, homemade cornbread.

Frost had just lit the woodstove for Gramps and put on a teakettle to warm water for hot chocolate. He joined her as Gramps gave each of them their food and they returned to the family room. Zoey seated herself on the couch, and Frost set his bowl on the coffee table next to where she was, then went to light the fire in the hearth.

He'd obviously had years of practice because the kindling caught on the first try, bringing the crackling fire to life.

Even though there were other people in the room—Nan, Gramps and the babies—the dark room lit only with the flicker of the firelight gave the room an intimate ambience, especially because Nan and Gramps were talking quietly together as if they were alone in the room, leav-

ing Zoey and Frost to have their own conversation. There
was room between them on the couch, but she could feel
Frost's presence as if there was no space at all. She took
a deep breath and forced herself to turn her attention to
the twins.

Ari was working on her consonant-vowel combinations
in the background, and Dante had fallen sound asleep with
his fist in his mouth.

Zoey finished her meal and pulled her legs up under
her, cupping the mug of hot cocoa Frost had made her.
She inhaled its dark-chocolate scent and savored the sight
of the mini marshmallows bobbing on top of the steam-
ing liquid.

For maybe the first and only time since she'd been at-
tacked in the college dorm and had subsequently rejected
Frost's marriage proposal, she felt at peace. For tonight, at
least, she'd put aside the memory of her pathetic excuse
for an audition at the symphony. There wasn't anything
she could do about it now anyway. It wasn't as if she could
go back in time and play perfectly, without any mistakes.

When God closed a door, He opened a window, right?
She just had to have faith, look around and find the new
path the Lord would set out for her.

The way this evening was unfolding was more like
the life she'd dreamed about since she was a little girl—
a close family enjoying an evening together around the
warm hearth. The sounds of one baby babbling while the
other made sweet little snoring noises in his sleep was
music to her ears.

It was impossible to express a mother's love for her
children. Before the twins arrived, she hadn't imagined
it was conceivable for someone to love another person

so deeply. Sometimes she thought her heart could barely contain those feelings, and she wondered if Frost, as the twins' father, felt the same way.

From what she'd seen of his interactions with the babies, she thought he must. He clearly loved his offspring, however much of a surprise they'd been to him. The babies had been born out of their love. If only that love had lasted the test of time. If it had, what would their lives—and their love—be like now?

She took a sip of her hot cocoa, and it burned her lips, jolting her back to real life and out of her perfect little daydream. Hot chocolate made on a woodstove with boiling water was considerably warmer than straight out of a microwave, and she'd forgotten to blow on it first before swallowing a big gulp of the searing liquid and gooey marshmallows that burned all the way down her gullet.

With that sudden shock back to reality came the reminder of what was really happening this evening and not what she wanted it to be. It was a blizzard, and she was here with the twins because Frost had deemed it the safest place to be. That was all. All those sentimental emotions she'd just been experiencing—those were nothing more than a smokescreen. While she and Frost were the twins' parents and would therefore be part of each other's lives for as long as they lived, that was as far as their relationship went. A power outage and what felt to her like an intimate and romantic evening by a fire weren't going to change that reality.

Her eyes met Frost's and he offered her a grim smile. She wondered if he was thinking the same thing, how different they'd both planned for their lives to be. What would this evening look like if the attack hadn't happened, if she'd accepted Frost's proposal? Once she'd discovered she was pregnant, they'd probably have gotten married right away so the twins would have been born into a family with a mom and dad who were married to each other. Frost would have accepted no less, being the stand-up guy that he was.

But even that wouldn't have been a guarantee of happiness, and it was high time she accepted everything life had thrown at her. Things were what they were for a reason, even if only God knew what it was.

"Frost, why don't you play us a song on the piano?" Nan suggested, and Frost nearly jumped off the sofa in his haste to scramble over to the piano. Zoey knew that, in the same way it was for her, music was Frost's safe place, and she wondered what his thoughts had been just now that made him dash to the piano to escape them.

"What's your poison tonight, Nan? Country? Pop? Something classical?" he asked.

Zoey sighed, looking forward to the music. At least her migraine had faded. Stress was usually one of her biggest triggers and she'd half expected to be bedridden in pain.

"Zoey, do you want to—" Gramps started, but Frost cut him off before he could complete the sentence, clearly anticipating what he'd been about to say.

Zoey was halfway to her feet, also anticipating Gramps's suggestion for her to accompany Frost with her violin, but she sat back down again when Frost spoke.

"No, Gramps. Please. It's been a long day. I want her to relax tonight while I impress her with my mad keyboarding skills." He darted a quick glance at Zoey and winced an unspoken apology.

Gramps gave a raspy grunt and shook his head. "Watch

that ego, son, or your head is going to swell up like a balloon."

Zoey already knew Frost was an accomplished piano
player, but she was more grateful than she could express
for the reprieve. He was incredibly thoughtful and knew
her so well. After the day she had, the last thing she
wanted to do was pull out her violin and play right now,
even if it was a completely different genre than the classical piece she'd played earlier in the day. The pain and
embarrassment of her audition was far too fresh, and she
was afraid she'd make a mess out of anything she tried to
play tonight. Or else she'd burst into fresh tears and have
to explain every humiliating detail to Nan and Gramps,
which was another thing she didn't want to do. Either
way, she was grateful Frost had nipped it in the bud and
saved her the agony.

"Opera," Nan said, ignoring the sudden tension in the
room, or perhaps speaking over it on purpose. Nan was
sensitive that way. "And I want you to sing. In Italian, luv.
Give us a famous tenor aria, if you please."

Dante awoke and started to fuss, so Zoey picked him
up and perched him on her lap with his bottle, which he
slurped noisily. She was as eager as Nan to hear Frost play
and sing. In Zoey's opinion, opera was an odd choice for
a cabin in the woods during a blackout, but it was nothing Frost couldn't accommodate with ease. She happened
to love opera herself, and she suspected his babies would
enjoy his smooth voice as much as she did.

Gramps took Ari, who was happy just sitting with him
and amusing herself by pulling on his scraggly beard.

"Seriously, Nan? Opera? Not an Irish folk song or old-
time country?" Frost asked.

Zoey was secretly hoping for the tenor aria. Frost had an amazing range, not to mention a richness of tone that would make any woman melt—especially when he sang in Italian.

Chapter Twelve

Frost closed his eyes and started playing. The piano was nothing more than an ancient upright that had definitely seen better days and was perhaps not one hundred percent tuned on key, and yet Frost did his best to make the plunky old thing sound as if he were playing on a baby grand.

He sang the first line and then stopped, shook his head and cleared his throat.

"Sorry. I didn't warm up first," he apologized, singing a couple of quick scales. "You can't just jump into an opera aria like that without warming up your voice."

"You're so good I could happily listen to you *just* sing scales," Zoey remarked with a smile. "Or the phone book."

He couldn't help that his ego inflated with her words of praise. Despite their current situation, his love song was for her alone.

The second time he started the song, he was immediately lost in the story behind the lyrics. In opera, the tenors were usually the good guys, but they rarely succeeded at winning the loves of their lives. Most of the time the plot twists got the best of them.

Kind of like him.

And if that wasn't bad enough, it seemed to him as if Zoey was the tragic romantic heroine. Yes, she'd turned down his proposal, but he was now certain he didn't know the whole story behind why she'd done so, and until he did, he couldn't move forward with his own life.

He'd been waiting for her to open up to him on her own since she'd first returned to Whispering Pines, but as of yet, she hadn't admitted why she had not accepted his offer. It couldn't have come as that much of a surprise, and he'd thought at the time it would have been a good one.

He sang the last line of the aria with gusto and finished the piece, then paused with his hands still hovering over the keys.

After a moment of complete silence, his captive audience applauded, even the babies, with Zoey and Gramps's help.

Nan stood and yawned. "I think Gramps and I are going to call it a night and leave you two young'uns to put the babies down for the evening."

After he wished Gramps and Nan a pleasant evening, Frost grabbed a bottle from the kitchen, warming it for a moment using a pan of hot water from the woodstove and carefully testing the temperature of the formula on the inside of his wrist.

He was really looking forward to the opportunity to put the babies down for the night. It would be a first for him, and he was glad Zoey was here to help out in case he forgot something.

She'd been running him through specifics ever since he'd found out he was a father—*daddy lessons*, she called them—and putting the twins to bed was a big one. He had no clue what they needed to fall into a deep sleep.

"Do you remember which twin likes to do what as we put them down for sleep?" Zoey asked.

Ugh. He *didn't* remember. He shook his head.

"Dante eats his way to sleep, and Ari likes to be rocked and sung to while she's patted on her back. Of course, I've been the one singing to her, and I'm not nearly as good as you are. I'll bet she'll drop off even faster when you're the one singing."

"Stop that," Frost said, lowering his brow. He hated it when she got down on herself. She never used to be that way. Back when they'd first started dating, she'd been such a confident young woman. That self-assurance was part of what had attracted him to her, and it was also what had made him so certain she'd accept his proposal.

But ever since that time, Zoey seemed to be constantly second-guessing herself.

What had changed?

He stared at her, taking her measure and trying to figure out the answers to his unspoken questions.

"What?" she asked, shaking her head and looking confused.

"I don't like to hear you talking down about yourself. You have a pretty voice, and you know it. Plus, I know voice lessons were part of your training for your bachelor's degree. And you're the twins' mom. Of course, they're going to love your voice."

"You're still better," she insisted. "Do you want to switch babies?"

"No, I do not," he said in a grave monotone, wishing she would believe what he was telling her. *He* wanted to hear her sing, and he knew Ari did, too. "I want to spend some time with my son right now."

"Maybe that's just as well for your first night helping put the twins to sleep. Dante is a little easier to put down.

Once his little tummy is full and he's had a good burp, he'll be sound asleep. Nothing will wake him up until it's time to eat again."

Frost settled in the armchair and fed Dante while Zoey rocked Ari back and forth in her arms, singing a lilting Irish folk song Frost remembered as being one of her favorites.

"See? You have a wonderful voice," he whispered as Ari drifted to sleep on Zoey's shoulder. "I love listening to you, and clearly it has the same effect on Ari."

"Yes, Ari has dozed off. Looks like Dante has, as well. Ready to put them down for the evening?" she murmured, ignoring his compliment.

He nodded. Dante was now dead weight, his bottle having dropped out of his mouth, and his only movement the occasional noisy sucking of his fist. Frost stood and took an LED lantern off the kitchen table, then led the way down the hall to his bedroom, which was currently also being used as the nursery, where they carefully laid the babies in their portable cribs.

"You can stay here in my room tonight and I'll take the couch in the living room," he offered. "Feel free to come get me if you need help with the babies any time during the night."

"Sounds good," she said. "I appreciate the offer. But do you mind if I sit by the hearth for a little while longer? It's been a really tough day and I just want to relax for a bit."

"Absolutely, I don't mind at all," he agreed, glad that she felt she could loosen up around him.

They both settled on the couch, and once again, Zoey curled her legs up underneath her. Daisy jumped up on the couch next to Zoey on the opposite side of where Frost was sitting and rested her muzzle on Zoey's leg with a contented doggy sigh.

"Traitor," Frost murmured.

"She probably just senses I need her more than you do right now. Emotional basket case right here." She pointed to herself with both index fingers, twirling them around in the universal sign for crazy.

Frost reached out and took Zoey's hand in his, running his thumb across the soft, smooth skin on the back of her hand.

"I know it was a rough day for you. Do you want to tell me about it?"

She sighed and turned her hand over, linking their fingers. "I've never felt so anxious over an audition before. I don't know why. I've done many auditions in the past with no problem. I guess my nerves got the best of me. Maybe because it was so important to me."

Frost remained silent, allowing her to get the whole story out.

"How many times a day do I practice my scales, something I've done ever since elementary school? They are totally second nature to me, to the point where I don't even have to think about what I'm doing. There's no reason for me to flub a single note. And then I'm in the middle of auditioning for the symphony and I flub them? I missed a half step and had to go back and repeat that part."

She inhaled audibly, and it sounded as if she was holding back tears. "And then there was my classical piece. I know that song inside and out and practiced it until I knew it by heart, though I had the music right in front of me. There was just no excuse for what happened. When I missed a note, instead of ignoring it and just continuing on as a professional musician would do, I stopped and apologized. *Stopped and apologized.* Way to highlight my mistakes," she said with a groan as tears flooded her eyes.

Frost's heart broke for her, knowing how much she wanted this dream. "Maybe it wasn't as bad as it felt at the time," he gently suggested. "It can't have been the first time the judges had something like that happen."

"I. Stopped. Playing," she repeated, enunciating each word. "Right in the middle of the piece. You just don't do that. Not if you're a professional. And if the judges have seen that before, they've written a big, fat fail on the audition form."

He shook his head. "I get what you're saying, though I really hope they saw through that one moment and heard the rest of your music for what it was. You have such an extraordinary gift."

"I wish."

"I don't think you ought to let what happened today define you. One bad audition doesn't make you *not* a professional."

"I know. And before you say it, I understand I still have plenty of options for my future, even if I've blown my first choice. All I can do is put it in the past and figure out what my future will look like going forward."

He made a scratchy sound from the back of his throat. "That makes two of us. But the bright side is we have Dante and Ari, right? They have their whole lives ahead of them, and we'll both be blessed to be a part of it."

"It's a lot different from the way we had everything planned back when we were in high school, but it's not all bad," she agreed.

They sat in silence for a long time, staring into the fire, each lost in their own thoughts but still holding hands.

"Why did you pick Tosca tonight?" she asked, barely above a whisper, referring to the opera aria he'd sung.

He met her gaze and held it. He knew exactly why he'd made the selection he had, and it had nothing to do with pleasing Nan and everything to do with Zoey.

Had she got the message?

"Why do you think?" Frost asked, his voice lower and huskier than usual. His gaze caught and held hers, his eyes darkening to glinting silver.

"Hmm," said Zoey, tilting her head and biting her bottom lip but not breaking his gaze. She took a deep breath and began reciting the lyrics in English.

"And the stars were shining
And the earth was smelling
The orchard gate creaked
And a footstep grazed the sand
She entered, fragrant
She fell into my arms."

"You should probably stop there before he starts going on about having to die," he said with a laugh. "You know how these opera lyrics go."

"I love opera. Especially the tenor arias. Everything sounds so romantic in Italian. I enjoy other foreign languages in opera as well, and even English, but Italian is definitely my favorite musical language."

Still holding her gaze and her hand, he leaned closer.

"Elucevan le stelle
Ed olezzava la terra
Stridea l'uscio dell'orto."

The words were every bit as romantic spoken in his rich voice as they had been when sung. Maybe more so. She drew in an audible breath as he offered her a soft,

"Eun passo sfiorava la rena
Entrava ella, fragrante
Mi cadea, fra le braccia."

By the time he finished, his voice was a whisper, and their foreheads were nearly touching, but he still held her gaze.

He pulled in a ragged breath. "I really want to kiss you right now, but…"

She knew what he was saying even without the words. *I proposed to you. You turned me down.*

Of course, he didn't think he could make the first move. Not now.

And even though at the time, turning down his offer of marriage had been the only thing she could do because of where she'd been emotionally, so many things had changed since then. She had become a parent to the twins, and her personal relationship with Frost had grown since she'd come back to Whispering Pines. As her heart squeezed tightly within her, she realized that despite everything, her feelings for him had never really changed.

Not deep down.

They still had a huge bridge to cross to get anywhere close to meeting in the middle. Or, if she was being honest with herself, she felt as if that bridge must mostly, if not entirely, be broached by her. She had much further to walk than he, and it was up to her to take the first steps.

Could it start here tonight?

Frost hadn't moved, and his gaze was deep and unreadable.

She unlinked her fingers from his and framed his face with both hands, her fingers brushing the outline of his strong jaw as she felt his light beard under her palms.

She had so much she wanted to say.

But not now.

She leaned in slowly until their lips touched, just barely.

Frost wrapped his arms around her and kissed her back.

"I've been wanting to do that for a long time," Frost admitted, surrounding her with his strong arms. "Even after—" His voice clogged with emotion.

She knew she had put this moment off for too long. Even though her gut tightened and rolled as if she were on a roller coaster, she was not going to kiss him and then run away without explaining the past.

She turned in his arms, so he was still holding her, but they were sitting face-to-face.

"I need to tell you something," she admitted, her voice cracking with strain. She could feel a migraine coming back. "It's something I should have told you a long time ago."

Chapter Thirteen

Frost could see what it was costing her to speak, and he knew that he needed to know what it was she wanted to share—whatever it was she'd been keeping from him all this time. But he didn't want this moment to end.

"You don't have to tell me," he said, his words tumbling out. She could tell him…

Eventually.

He tried to close the distance between them, but she pushed him back with her palms.

"Yes, I do have to talk to you," she insisted. "Now. Frost, I need you to listen to me. Please don't make this harder than it already is."

His heart was beating painfully loud in his ears, so much so that he could barely hear what she was saying, but he blew out a shaky breath and scrubbed a hand through his hair.

"Go ahead," he said, his voice low and raspy. "I'm listening."

"Okay." She dropped her gaze from his and reached out to pet Daisy, her eyes glued to the responsive canine. "I want to tell you why I turned down your proposal."

She took a deep breath, then began to speak. "It all started the night we were together. It really confused me.

You were the one who'd pressed so hard to wait until marriage. I thought it was a faith thing, a God thing with you."

He winced.

His decision to wait for marriage *had* been a faith thing, and that one night he'd spent with Zoey had been him being rebellious, blatantly turning his back on God's love, yet still believing it would all work out in the end.

Worse yet, Zoey had been a new Christian at the time, and he'd led her down the wrong path rather than being the man of God she should have had at her side.

"I know it sounds stupid now," he said, "but I justified my actions that night because I'd already bought you an engagement ring and was just waiting for the perfect time to ask you to marry me."

"I didn't know that. You didn't say," she whispered, her voice cracking with strain.

He laughed without mirth. "It was supposed to be a surprise."

"Oh, it was that. You caught me totally off guard when you proposed."

"A *good* surprise," he amended, clamping his jaw against the pain churning through his gut.

"I was just so angry at you, Frost. Maybe that wasn't fair of me, but that was how I felt. I know I was just as responsible as you were. I was every bit a willing participant that night. But I was trying to justify my actions and make you the villain, so I didn't have to take accountability for myself."

"I guess I can understand that. I was angry at myself, as well, for losing my moral compass that way. But that still doesn't explain the twins, Zoey. You were angry with me because you blamed me for our night together, and because of that you turned down my proposal. I don't like it, but I get it. Yet, then you found out you were pregnant. They may have been, and are, my babies, and you didn't even so much as call me to let me know. Didn't you think I deserved to know I might be a father?" The pain in his heart burst forth through his voice.

"If that was all that had happened, then of course I would have reached out to you as soon as I tested positive. But there is a lot more you don't know that made the whole situation untenable."

The atmosphere had changed again. Frost felt Zoey pulling into herself and Daisy immediately alerted, scooting closer to her and bumping her with her soft muzzle.

Frost's shoulders tightened and he thought his heart may have stopped beating altogether. Whatever Zoey was about to tell him, this was the *real* story, the one he had sensed was there all along and that he'd been waiting for her to share.

"Like I said, I was so angry after our time together, at you and at myself. I was afraid we'd ruined our relationship. And I was worried that things would never be the same between us."

She took a deep breath and let it out on a sob. This was so, so hard to talk about. She'd thought with time it would be better, but in many ways, the longer she waited, the worse it had become. She took another deep breath and began.

"My dorm was having a party. I usually just stayed in my room, putting on headphones to block out the noise. But I guess I was too amped up that night and just wanted to forget about everything for a while."

He reached for her hand. "Honey, I don't blame you for a moment of weakness. We all have them."

She pulled her hand back as if he'd burned her.

"No. No. It wasn't like that at all."

"Tell me, then." He sounded calm and collected despite how worked up she was.

"I was so stupid!" she burst out, not even trying to hide her tears anymore. "I only had one drink, and I didn't even drink very much of that one. I'd left it on an end table where I'd been sitting while I visited the restroom. It didn't even occur to me that someone might mess with my drink. My mind was whirling with too many thoughts about what had happened between us. I wasn't paying enough attention to my surroundings.

"I was only gone a few minutes. And I only took a few more sips of my drink when I returned. Then I started feeling funny. Within minutes I was feeling even worse."

"You'd been drugged?"

She nodded.

"Oh, honey, I'm so sorry. Did you know at the time that there was something seriously off with you?"

"Well, like I said, I felt funny. Odd. But it's not like I really had anything to compare it with, since I'd never been drunk before, or even tipsy. I figured it must just be the alcohol in my system, and I mentally berated myself because it had been a stupid idea to go to the party and drink. So, I decided to go back to my room.

"I was having a hard time walking straight and was slurring my words. I just wanted to go lie down and hide. Somehow, I got back to my room, but…"

Tears poured down her cheeks as the memory washed over her.

"I immediately passed out on my bed. And when I woke up, I wasn't alone. There was a strange man in my room—someone I didn't know from school. Thankfully, the door was wide open, and a male friend from across the hall happened to walk by. He saw the guy in my room, took one look at my expression and kicked the stranger out, asking me over and over again if I was okay."

Frost wrapped his arms tightly around her, and this time she didn't protest. She'd expected him to be walking away from her right about now, but instead he was comforting her.

She should have known. Frost had such a tender heart.

"Honey," he whispered in a gravelly voice, pressing a kiss into her hair. "This is all my fault. You wouldn't have been at that party if it weren't for me failing to act like a man of faith. I completely let you down."

"It was never your fault," she assured him, covering his arms with hers, reveling in the strength that was Frost. "And anyway, that's not why I felt I had to bring this to light."

"What, then?" Frost said, appearing to miss the point entirely.

"You've asked me on numerous occasions why I didn't call you the moment I found out I was pregnant with the twins. Well, first, I was too ashamed, not only by what we'd done but by what had happened afterward. And honestly, Frost, since I'd lost consciousness that night in the dorm, it was possible that Dante and Ari were..."

Frost stiffened, made a fist and punched the air.

"Dante and Ari are yours," she said quietly. "No matter what I may or may not have suffered through, those babies are one hundred percent yours. I don't need a DNA test to prove that."

"And I will be there to love and protect them *always*," he vowed.

Frost framed her face with his palms and leaned down to brush his lips over hers. She closed her eyes, enjoying the moment even while knowing it would probably never happen again. Frost was comforting her in the best way he knew how. She wanted to imprint the moment in her memory forever to lean on whenever things got rough in the future.

"Zoey," Frost whispered over her mouth. "Open your eyes, honey."

She did as he asked and as her heart roared to life, she read all the varied emotions in his gaze. So much tenderness, but there was pain there as well, and she knew she'd caused that.

"I may not have been the man you needed me to be back then, but I still wish you would have told me what had happened. I would have been there for you no matter what. We could have gotten married right away, and I would have been able to support you through the whole thing. I can't imagine all the darkness you ended up facing all alone."

Just then, Dante let out a wail that startled them both. She hadn't realized they'd been talking so deep into the night.

"He's still doing a night feeding, the little chunky monkey," she explained, pulling away from Frost.

"I'll bank the fire," Frost said.

Would Frost have said more? That he was committed to being strong co-parents together? She already knew that. She'd known that when she'd first come to town to seek him out.

Or could it be he'd been about to say there was hope for something more in the future?

But now she might never know what he'd been about to say.

Chapter Fourteen

The electricity came back on sometime in the night, and by morning the sun was shining, making the white sheet of snow outside glisten. With Nan and Gramps's help, Frost was able to not only cover the twins' morning changing and feeding while Zoey slept, but also to start making a breakfast of pancakes, scrambled eggs and hash browns, his specialty.

Oh, who was he trying to kid? Breakfast wasn't his specialty. It was the only meal he knew how to make. If it wasn't cold cuts, peanut butter and jelly, or something he could pop in the microwave, he was pretty much toast.

Oh, yeah. *Toast*. He could do that, too.

"Good morning," he greeted cheerfully as Zoey scuffled into the kitchen, yawning behind her palm and looking adorably ruffled.

"I didn't even hear the babies wake this morning," she said, shaking her head in amazement. "Why didn't you get me up?"

"We figured you deserved to sleep in for a change," Frost said with a grin, pulling out a chair at the kitchen table and gesturing her into it. "Take a seat. I've almost got breakfast finished for you."

She wiped her eyes dramatically. "Am I hallucinating here? I don't smell toast, so I don't think I'm having a stroke."

"Ha, ha. If you aren't nice to me, I may not share my pancakes with you." He remembered their comfortable banter from their past. It used to be this way all the time, and he couldn't help but want it to be that way again. And he didn't care that Gramps and Nan were looking on with wide-eyed curiosity and amusement.

"Pancakes?" Zoey's eyes brightened.

"With chocolate chips in them. Your favorite, as I recall." He flipped a couple of pancakes onto a plate and presented it to her with a flourish.

"This looks delicious," she said, scooping a spoonful of scrambled eggs and hash browns from a nearby platter onto her plate before digging in.

"Don't speak too soon," Gramps warned with a grunt. "You haven't tasted it yet. This is Frost we're talking about, not some fancy chef."

"Ouch," Frost said, gripping at his chest over his heart. "What is this? Roast Frost Day?"

"It's fun. We all know you can take it," Zoey said. "And for the record, these pancakes are delicious. You could open a restaurant with these—or at least a diner."

"Yeah?" After serving Nan and Gramps, he grabbed his own plate and sat down opposite Zoey. He was busy cutting up his pancakes and drowning them in genuine maple syrup when he felt Zoey's eyes on him.

He looked up and met her curious gaze.

"What?" he asked. "Do I have a hair out of place or something?"

"Your curls always look messy," she assured him with a laugh. "No, it's something else I'm wondering about."

"Yeah? What, then?"

"Well, this morning I noticed a half-finished application for the University of Northern Colorado on your desk. It surprised me because I thought you'd already sent it in. I promise I wasn't snooping or anything. It was right on top of a pile of papers."

"Humph." He shook his head. "I was trying to write a decent essay and was really struggling with it. I've never been the greatest writer, especially essays. Why do they have to be so random? *Recount a time when you faced a challenge, setback or failure. How did it affect you, and what did you learn from the experience?* Ugh. I'm glad I didn't put any more time into it than I already have. What a waste."

"Why is that? Have you decided to go to a different college? I know you're aware teaching and music are both major strengths at UNC."

"No. It's not that I want to go somewhere else. I definitely wanted to attend UNC. I always have, ever since high school, which I guess you know better than most, since we'd originally planned to go together."

"What, then? I'm confused."

He raised his eyebrows. As if it weren't obvious. Surely she hadn't missed that his sentence used the past tense.

"It's on the back burner."

Again.

He didn't have to say that part aloud. He also didn't have to say that this dream had probably permanently passed him by. He couldn't even look her in the eyes.

"Why?" she asked, her voice suddenly hardening.

He looked around the table. Nan and Gramps were keeping their opinions to themselves for a change, maybe because both of the usually outspoken individuals were busy playing with the babies they were holding and were intentionally not paying attention to the conversation.

The babies were the very reason Frost had nixed the idea of going to college now. He had other responsibilities to uphold.

"The twins," he said aloud. "I need to be working full time to take care of them, and I want to be around them as much as possible, which I can't do if I'm off at college."

"You've always encouraged me to reach for my dreams," Zoey reminded him, and then scoffed. "Although we all know how that turned out for me."

She dropped her silverware onto her plate with a clatter, then stood, her expression bleak. "I need a breath of fresh air."

She didn't wait for Frost to acknowledge her comment before making a beeline for the mud room, grabbing her winter coat off the hook by the door and an extra pair of snow boots left by Frost's sisters as she went.

For a long moment, Frost just stared after her.

"What are you waiting for, boy?" Gramps asked in a gravelly tone. "You know what to do. Go after her."

Frost glanced around, feeling dazed. Of course, Zoey was still upset about yesterday's audition. It would take some time for her to get over that. But what could he say to encourage her that he hadn't already said?

There were plenty of other opportunities here in Colorado for a violinist of Zoey's talent and skill. She just needed to broaden her horizons.

"Right," he said, rising and threading his arms into his jean jacket. "Can you guys watch the twins for a few minutes?"

"Go," Nan said. "The babies will be fine."

Frost exited the ranch house, unsure where Zoey would have gone but knowing she probably hadn't gone far, what with the two fresh feet of snow the blizzard had dumped on the ground. It would have been hard for her to walk very far, so he should easily be able to follow her footsteps.

As he expected, she hadn't left the porch. She was standing next to the swing, her arms tightly wrapped around herself against the bite of the cold wind as she stared off into the distance.

"Zoey?" he whispered, not wanting to startle her, and then again louder when she didn't respond.

When he reached her side, he could see the tears pouring down her cheeks as she sobbed quietly, her face red from crying and the cold air.

"Zoey, what…?" Was it the botched audition that was breaking her heart, or something else? A lot had happened in the last twenty-four hours, leaving him with far more questions than answers. He opened his arms to her, but when he tried to touch her, she pulled away, curling into herself even more.

"Zoey?" he asked again, his voice low and husky from worry.

"Don't," she snapped, surprising him with her intensity. "Don't make me the reason you walk away from your dreams. Finish your application. Go to UNC. You deserve it."

"I have a good life here on the farm and a job I enjoy, which is better than most people can say. I get to sing and play my guitar at Sally's every Friday night, as well as at family bonfires. And I have the twins." He paused, men-

tally tripping over the words he hadn't said. *I have you.*
Because he didn't yet know what that meant. He took a
deep breath and continued. "I don't need more than that
to be happy."

"And yet it's not what you really want."

"I *want* to take care of the twins. I need to be working
full time to do that."

She tilted her head up at him, her eyes filled with disbelief.

What was she getting at?

"I was up most of the night thinking about it," she admitted. "My plan B hasn't changed, Frost. If I can't play in
the Colorado Symphony Orchestra, I want to give myself
the opportunity to try working on Broadway."

"New York City? Still? But I thought… I'd hoped…
After everything…" He could barely speak around the
lump in his throat and the simultaneous breaking of his
heart.

He didn't know why he'd assumed things had changed.
She'd told him of her plans on the first night she'd returned
to Whispering Pines, so he shouldn't be so shocked that
she still intended to follow her dreams wherever they led
her. He remembered how enthralled she'd been with New
York City when they visited during their senior year class
trip in high school, and how completely overwhelmed he'd
felt by all the people and the noise. He hadn't been a city
boy back then and he never would be.

Yet somehow, after they'd spent so much time together
recently—him, Zoey and the twins—

Maybe not *family*, exactly, but something like it. How
could she think for a moment he wouldn't want the chil-

dren in his life on a regular basis? That he'd even accept that scenario?

But was it fair to deny her the opportunity to do what she wanted with her life, even if that meant she and the twins would be going far away? Could he really add to her stress by fighting her on that?

Yet, how could he not? How could he live his life as an absentee father whose twins barely knew him?

Trying to convince her to choose a life in Colorado would be the same as her suggesting he follow her to New York City knowing it wasn't for him. They were at an impasse.

After last night, he'd thought they were growing closer, but it obviously hadn't been enough.

Or perhaps it had been too much.

There was no *fair*.

Zoey could see by the look on his face that she'd hurt Frost with her words.

Of course she had. None of this was fair to him.

She couldn't imagine anyone telling her they were going to take Dante and Ari away from her, far across the country where she couldn't even visit them regularly. But if she and the twins weren't here, they wouldn't be holding him back from his dreams. He could get on with his life and attend college as he'd intended to before she'd shown up and blown everything to bits.

Wasn't that important, too?

Frost would be a big part in his kids' lives no matter where they lived. Zoey would make sure of that, at whatever cost. And she knew Frost would, too. They would make it work. They had to.

But those kids in middle school, the ones who would benefit from Frost following his dreams and getting his degree? They needed a teacher like Frost, someone whose very soul radiated music and who could relate to kids and teenagers.

And Frost needed them, too.

Whether he knew it or not, the best thing for him was for her to leave. She just didn't know how to tell him that so he would believe it.

"You know I'll plan to take regular time off during the year between playing for shows so I can bring the babies back to Whispering Pines to visit you. And we will have phone calls and video calls every night. I promise the twins won't forget you're their father."

His eyes shone with unshed tears, and he rubbed them away with his thumb and forefinger.

"When do you plan to go?"

"I'm not sure yet. I didn't really make any concrete plans when I thought I'd probably be—well, that idea has come to nothing, hasn't it?"

"You don't know that yet," he reminded her, his voice harsh.

But she *did* know. She'd made an utter disaster of her audition. The only thing she could do now was put it behind her and look to the future—New York City with all its Broadway and off-Broadway shows and musicals. Surely she could find work at one of the theaters there.

She reached up and brushed her palm across Frost's scruffy jaw, then brushed a soft kiss over his lips. "Thank you for that."

She left him on the porch, staring off into the distance.

Somehow, she knew he wouldn't follow her back inside right away.

Which was a good thing. Because she had something she needed to do.

"Can you give me another minute?" she asked Nan as she returned to the kitchen after taking off her snow boots and hanging her coat in the mudroom.

"Sure, sweetie. Take whatever time you need."

Nan clearly thought she was asking for more time to get her emotions together, but right now Zoey had something else on her mind. She rushed down the hallway toward Frost's room. She didn't know how much time she had, so she needed to make it quick.

The application for UNC was where she'd left it after she looked at it earlier. She stared at it for a moment, wondering if she should go ahead with her plan. Maybe this was a bad idea. If it was, it was a *very* bad idea. Frost was either going to appreciate her more or never talk to her again, metaphorically speaking.

It was a risk she was going to have to take, for Frost's sake.

She opened the diaper bag sitting on the changing table and carefully tucked the application inside, then took a deep, ragged breath. She jumped when she heard the door to the mudroom slam, indicating that Frost had returned inside, even though it would take him time to shed his coat and boots. He wouldn't suspect what she'd done. Anyway, she was doing this for him. So why did she feel so guilty?

She fished her cell phone out of her jean pocket and scrolled to Frost's sister Avery's number, pressing the call button.

"Hey, Avery," she said when Avery picked up. "This is Zoey. I was wondering if you and your sisters could meet with me at your bed and breakfast. I have a favor to ask you."

Chapter Fifteen

Frost stood leaning on the corral fence, one foot on the rail, staring at nothing, his mind a thousand miles away.

Zoey was going away. And she was taking the twins with her.

His heart wasn't just breaking. It had been shattered into a million pieces, even worse than when he'd proposed to Zoey, and she'd turned him down. He'd never recovered from that. Not really. So how was he supposed to live with this new reality?

He should have known better than to hope, to let himself grow close to Zoey again. He should have realized it would all end in heartbreak for him.

After returning Zoey and the kids to her mom's house, he'd come back to the farm and spent the day doing chores—hard, physical work to distract him from his feelings.

It hadn't worked. No matter how hard he toiled, he couldn't keep his mind from spinning. And yet for all that, he hadn't come up with a single answer to his dilemma.

She was moving to New York City, and he was staying at the farm to work to provide for his children—children he wouldn't see grow up. It was bad enough that he was losing the love of his life, but not getting to be a part of his children's lives was too much to bear.

Frost jumped at the sound of his brother's voice from just behind him, and Daisy barked a late welcome.

"Some guard dog you are," Frost told the beagle. "You're supposed to bark before the bad guy sneaks up on me."

"Bad guy?" Sharpe snorted. "It's a good thing I'm your loving brother, then, and not someone out to do you harm. And give poor Daisy a break. She's a hound dog for pity's sake, not a guard dog."

Frost chuckled. "She could have at least bayed at you so I would have known you were coming."

"I'm not so sure you would have heard her even if she had. Man, you were totally out there somewhere," Sharpe commented, coming up to lean on the fence next to him, his eyes narrowing as he took in Frost's measure. "I seriously called your name three times, and you didn't so much as budge."

Frost didn't bother trying to deny it. He and Sharpe had always been close. As the older brother, Sharpe had always watched out for Frost and would know if something was wrong. And since there *was* something wrong...

"Yeah," Frost acknowledged, hoping Sharpe wouldn't ask for more. Frost wasn't sure he could talk about it without completely losing it, which was the last thing he needed right now, especially in front of his big brother.

Please don't let him go there.

"What's up?"

Frost cringed.

He'd gone there.

Of course, he had. There was no way out. Even if he wanted to, which he didn't, Frost couldn't lie, especially not to his brother. Sharpe would pick up on that immediately. And he wouldn't stand for anything less than the whole truth, either.

"You're standing outside in freezing weather and not moving an inch to try to keep warm. Your nose is going to freeze and fall off if you aren't careful."

Frost scoffed. It wasn't exactly a laugh, which he was certain was the reaction his brother had been after, but Sharpe grinned anyway.

"It's Zoey and the twins," he admitted, his breath visible in the frigid air.

"Well, that much I could have guessed without your assistance, since they've been first and foremost in your mind since the moment they came to town. What about them?"

"They're leaving."

Sharpe's eyebrows rose in surprise. "Really? I thought you guys were getting along great. All of us even suspected maybe..." He didn't finish his sentence. He didn't need to.

His family wanted the best for Frost. They'd seen him mourn his relationship with Zoey when she'd turned down his proposal, watched him grieve for the breakdown of his life, and he knew they'd been scrutinizing him with hawk eyes when Zoey had returned to town with the twins.

Sharpe cleared his throat. "When?"

"I don't know. Soon, I guess. She has no reason to stick around. She's positive she bombed her audition with the Colorado Symphony and won't be asked to join. She isn't even going to wait for callbacks to confirm her suspicions. She's already pivoted to her plan B and is well on her way to leaving."

"Plan B? Which is?"

"She intends to go to New York and work on Broadway."

"Wow. I don't have to ask how you feel about that." Sharpe pressed his palm to Frost's shoulder and squeezed reassuringly. "I'm really sorry, bro. Is there anything at all I can do for you?"

Frost scoffed and shook his head. "Somehow make everything different so Zoey will stay?"

"Hmm," said Sharpe, scratching the scruff on his jaw. "You know, as much as I'd like to, I'm not the one who can do that for you guys. But maybe you can, if you put your mind to it."

"What's that supposed to mean?"

"Well, you said she hasn't actually heard from the symphony. So is it for sure a hard no?"

"I don't think so. I believe she'll at least make callbacks. I really do, though she's not banking on it. And she's not waiting, either."

"But she might stay if she was offered a place in the symphony. Maybe there *is* something you can do."

"Like what?" He believed in the power of prayer, but God didn't necessarily always answer prayers exactly the way he wanted Him to. It felt presumptuous to ask God to make such changes in their lives.

"I'm not sure, but there must be something. Do you know anyone who can put a good word in for her?"

"After the fact? Maybe, although I think it would have been better if it came before her audition instead of afterward."

"Who do you have in mind?"

"Her college symphony orchestra director might give her a recommendation. I know they had a good relationship. I'm sure she was on Zoey's resumé, but I don't know whether or not they actually phoned the references. It wouldn't hurt to reach out and ask her to make a call on Zoey's behalf."

"That's a good start," said Sharpe, leaning back so he could look Frost straight in the eyes, "but I think *you* ought to call the director as well."

"Me? Why? I'm a nobody. Nothing more than an ex-boyfriend and her baby daddy." He knew he sounded bitter but couldn't help himself. "I'd do her more harm than good."

"You are *so* not just her baby daddy. That's a terrible thing even to say," Sharpe snapped back, giving no quarter. "You've loved those twins and stepped up for them from the moment you discovered their existence."

Frost sighed. "You're right, of course. Sorry."

"And you're not a nobody, either. You have a unique perspective on Zoey's career that no one else has. You literally watched her grow up from the time she started playing her instrument in elementary school. You saw the way she flourished in high school as first chair in every band and orchestra she played in, and then watched her excel in college.

"Not to mention, you know her as a person as well as a musician. You know what a strong, determined woman she is. You've seen the way she's dedicated herself to her craft. You may be in the very best position to offer your opinion on what Zoey really has to offer. Maybe the director needs to hear that from you."

"You think?" Frost wasn't completely sold on the idea. Who was he to tell the director of the Colorado Symphony anything? A glorified karaoke singer? And what would Zoey think if she found out he was meddling in her affairs?

That wouldn't end well at all.

Then again, what if he could help her? What if he could give her a reason to remain in Colorado so he'd be able to stay with her and the twins? What if he *could* hand her her dreams on a platter?

"You've given me a lot to think and pray about," he said. "Thanks for your advice, bro. I appreciate it."

Sharpe slapped him on his bicep. "I'll be praying for you as well. Just don't think too long. Act while the acting is good."

"Yeah, I know. Thanks, again."

Sharpe nodded and moved away, whistling under his breath.

Frost turned and strode determinedly toward the house. He had some phone calls to make.

Zoey sat at a large table in Avery and Jake's bed and breakfast nervously nibbling on a corner of the best blueberry muffin she'd ever tasted. Having visited the bed and breakfast for a meal several times since she'd returned to Whispering Pines, she knew Jake was an amazing cook, but it was Ruby who'd brought her ex-marine husband Aaron's muffins to share today, and they were out-of-this-world amazing.

Jake, the twins' uncle, was watching Dante and Ari as well as his own brood in another room. He was a large, gregarious man, but a whiz with kids of all ages, and Zoey was completely confident in having the twins under his watchful eye.

Frost's four sisters and one sister-in-law all gathered

around her, chatting up a storm about everything happening in their daily lives since they'd last met, which hadn't been that long ago, since they worked together and saw one another nearly every day. Zoey was grateful for their steady friendship, and even more that they'd embraced her when she'd returned to town without judging her for what had happened between her and their brother. They had a lot to cast blame on her for, yet they'd chosen to take the high road where her relationship with Frost was concerned. If they had any opinions as to what had happened in the past, they kept them to themselves.

And that was exactly why she needed to talk with them about Frost today.

She needed their level-headed guidance. She'd been going back and forth on her plan, one minute certain it was the best idea in the world and the next thinking she was crazy for even considering it. What was best for Frost? And what if she was wrong?

She used to think she knew everything about Frost. But now, not so much.

"So," said Molly, curling a strand of hair behind her ear and leaning forward on her elbows on the table. "What can we do for you, Zoey? And remember, whatever you tell us stays between us, okay?"

Zoey smiled shakily. While kind, the Winslow sisters were formidable and straightforward. That was the very reason she'd come to them today. For what she was considering, she needed formidable and straightforward advice.

She opened the file folder in front of her and smoothed the papers with the palm of her hand.

All four sisters stopped speaking as they waited for

her to explain what she'd brought and what could be so important within the file folder.

Zoey's throat tightened and she cleared it apprehensively. "Before I begin, I ought to tell you that Frost doesn't know I have this," she started, her lips twitching into a nervous grin.

"*This* being?" Felicity asked with a sympathetic smile, voicing what all the sisters must be wondering. No one looked particularly surprised by Zoey's statement.

"Frost's application for the University of Northern Colorado."

Now the looks of astonishment spreading from sister to sister zapped around the room like a bolt of electricity.

Ruby's auburn eyebrows rose. "I have to say I'm surprised. That's great news. We didn't even know he was applying."

"Well, that's the thing. He's not. Or more accurately, he's not *now*. He intended to, until I showed up in town with the babies and ruined everything for him."

"I would hardly count bringing his twins to him as ruining his life," Avery countered. "It changed his focus, maybe, but that's not necessarily a bad thing. In my opinion, he's changed for the better since Dante and Ari came into his life."

"Yes, but it becomes a problem when it keeps him from following his dreams," Zoey said. "Don't you see?"

"Why have his plans changed?" Avery asked, and then blew on her coffee and took a tentative sip.

"You know your brother. He takes his responsibilities seriously, especially where his children are concerned. He intends to provide for his family, and in his mind that means keeping his full-time job here at the farm. I've tried to argue him out of it, but he's being particularly stubborn."

"Yeah, that noteworthy trait runs strong in the Winslow blood," Ruby said with a laugh. "Frost may be the sweetest of all of us, but he can still be just as stubborn."

"So, what are we going to do about it?" Avery asked, folding her hands on the table in front of her. Felicity reached out and squeezed Zoey's hand in solidarity.

She hadn't said *you*.

We.

Relief flooded through Zoey at Avery's matter-of-fact question. She'd given so much thought to it and prayed Frost's sisters would help, but even so, she was reassured by the way they appeared to be mentally circling the wagons around her with their support.

"I do have an idea," Zoey said, deciding to jump in with both feet. It was now or never. "But I'm not sure about it. Feel free to tell me if it's a huge mistake. I've been going back and forth on this for days and still can't decide if it's a good idea or not."

None of Frost's sisters interrupted her, so she took another deep breath, brushed her hair back with her fingers and charged in.

"I want to send his application in to the school."

"Without telling him you're doing it?" Avery asked.

Zoey met Avery's eyes, then moved her gaze from woman to woman around the table. "Yes."

"I think that's a great idea," Molly said, slapping her palms against the tabletop like a judge with a gavel.

"You do?" asked Zoey. She'd hoped for this answer but was still rather surprised by it.

"If you don't do it for him, he'll talk himself out of it," Felicity pointed out. "You know he will."

"In addition to submitting his application, I intend to look around for apartments so he has somewhere to stay in Greeley during the week for school, and then he can come home on weekends to work the farm. I thought that way he wouldn't feel as if he's completely abandoning his responsibility to his family—and yours."

Zoey was relieved by the number of nods and sounds of agreement going around the table.

"There is another thing, though," she continued. "Do you think Sharpe is going to mind taking over Frost's chores during the weekdays?"

Sharpe's wife Emma burst out laughing. "Oh, he's gonna mind, all right. Or at least he'll growl and grumble about it as if he was being put out because of it. But no worries. He can deal. I'll make sure of that."

"So, you think I should go ahead and send this in?" Zoey was still feeling shaky inside, still not a hundred percent sure about her choice, and she wanted additional confirmation, even though everyone was already smiling and nodding at her.

"Definitely," Frost's sisters said in chorus. "You should do it."

"And Frost isn't going to think I'm putting my nose where it doesn't belong?"

"You have a consensus here, Zoey," said Felicity gently. "If for some reason Frost gets angry about what you've done, we'll all take responsibility. He'd be foolish to go up against one strong woman who is doing what she thinks is best for him. But six? No man is that brave, and my brother knows better."

"Besides," said Avery practically. "Just because he'll be accepted into UNC doesn't mean he has to go. That's only the first step in the process. He'll have to audition to get into the music program, right?"

Zoey cringed inwardly at the word *audition*. "Good point. Not that it will be any real hurdle for him. He's a natural."

"Speaking of auditions," Ruby asked, "how did yours go?"

Zoey groaned and hid her face behind her palm. "Don't ask. It was bad."

"I'm sorry," said Felicity, running a hand across Zoey's shoulder. The other women murmured similar statements.

Zoey appreciated that they didn't try to condescend to her or to tell her she must be wrong. They simply accepted what she said at face value.

"That's the other thing I need to tell you," she said, knowing this part wasn't going to go over well. "Frost is really going to need your support during the next few months."

"Why?" asked Molly.

The quiet was suddenly deafening. "I'm going to be moving out of state soon. New York City. I'm going to try to play on Broadway."

There were murmurs and gasps around the table as everyone came to terms with what she'd just said. Not surprisingly, no one congratulated her on this decision.

"Poor Frost," Felicity whispered, her voice cracking with emotion. "He loves those babies." Zoey wasn't sure if she was meant to hear what Felicity had said, but she had, and it broke her heart.

"I know he does. And I'm sorry. I'll do everything I can

to be fair to Frost and his role as the father of the twins. But I have to try to make it work on Broadway. I fell in love with New York City when we visited for our high school senior trip, and it's always been my second choice after the Colorado Symphony. Since the first is a wash, I've just got to give it a go."

"What about having Frost move to New York?" Emma asked. She was the only one who hadn't grown up with Frost, so it was a logical question coming from her.

The women looked at one another around the table. Then Avery spoke for all the sisters. "We understand. Frost would be miserable in a big city, even if he did get to live near his family. It wouldn't be any good for him. He loves taking care of his animals."

"We promise we'll have Frost's back when the time comes." This vow came from Felicity, and Zoey's heart warmed.

That was the promise Zoey had been hoping to extract from them, but it didn't feel like enough.

Was she being selfish? Maybe. But she was legitimately thinking of Frost's best interests first. If she stayed here in Whispering Pines and found some other outlet for playing her violin, he wouldn't go to college. He just wouldn't. And that wouldn't be fair to him, either.

There were no objective answers. She'd thought this through, prayed about it, and cried about it until there were no tears left. No matter how painful this would be for everyone involved, it was the right thing to do.

If only there was another way.

Avery, seated on Zoey's left, reached out a hand to her. "Since we're all here together, let's bring this to the Lord."

One by one, the women took each other's hands. With

each connection, the bond around the table grew stronger. Women praying together and asking God for help—that was true power, more than the mightiest army. Zoey could feel the change in the room as each of Frost's sisters bowed their heads.

She'd come here today looking for advice from the smartest women she knew. But they'd known to reach out to Someone with even greater wisdom.

The Lord.

Chapter Sixteen

Arriving at the family bonfire with Daisy at his heels two weeks later, Frost found that Sharpe had prepped the logs and kindling in advance, so it was easy for him to light it up. Most evenings, family bonfires were an activity he most looked forward to, but this night was different, and one way or another, the outcome was going to change his life forever.

This was Zoey's going-away party, and despite all he had planned for the evening, he felt heavy inside. The little thread of hope he'd been grasping onto was feeling thinner by the moment. He still hoped that she would come to a different decision, that she'd choose to play her violin for somewhere regional or local. But she'd made her decision. She was going to move to New York City.

And he had one last opportunity to change her mind.

"I brought my fiddle," Zoey said from behind him, and he jerked so violently he almost fell into the blazing fire.

"I didn't hear you come up," he admitted, placing a palm on his racing heart.

"Yeah. You looked pretty lost in thought there. In your defense, though, I don't have the babies with me. If I had, you would have heard us coming from a mile away."

Frost offered her a soft smile, the best he could do at the moment. "Where are Dante and Ari, anyway?"

"Oh, they'll be along soon. Mom is bringing them. She's picking up Gramps and Nan. I thought maybe we could warm up with a couple of songs before everyone else gets here."

Frost straightened his spine and captured her gaze.

What was this?

One last hurrah? Was that what she was trying to tell him? That this would be the last time they ever played together? They never warmed up before they played or practiced together. The two of them had the amazing knack of being able to duet together majestically without the least bit of practice. They could follow each other, jumping from song to song without missing a note. It was as if they could read each other's minds.

Not anymore, though. He had no idea what she was trying to say to him.

But even if she moved to New York, she'd be back with the twins to visit from time to time, wouldn't she? And surely there would be other times for family bonfires. Or was she simply trying to emphasize how much things were going to change after today?

He swallowed hard. "Sure. Let me clean up my hands and we can play a couple of pieces."

He popped a couple of antibacterial wipes from a nearby container, washed the soot and grime from his hands, and then moved to his log to grab his guitar.

"So, what did you have in mind to practice?"

"Opera?" she teased. "I know Nan would appreciate it."

"At a campfire?" Frost chuckled.

"Let's sing some elementary songs, then."

"I'm not sure my brothers and sisters will appreciate kids' camp songs, but I'll humor you for now."

"Maybe not your brothers and sisters, but don't you think you ought to consider your nieces and nephews? I'm sure they'll like your repertoire."

"I'll have to dig deep. It's been a while on some of these." He plucked at a few strings, tuning the instrument, and then strummed a few chords.

Zoey, her violin tucked under her chin and her bow held at the ready, stared at him expectantly.

Frost dug around his mind for something he'd sung to the twins and after a moment broke out into "Mary Had a Little Lamb."

"Ah. No, no, no," Zoey broke in halfway through the first verse. "*What* do you think you're singing?"

"Um... I thought I was singing 'Mary Had a Little Lamb,'" he said wryly. "Why? What did you hear?"

"A funeral dirge in a minor key," she informed him. "You're either going to put all the kids into a coma state or make them cry."

His jaw dropped. "I—I—" he stammered.

"I'm kidding, Frost," she assured him. She turned to Jake and Avery, who'd just arrived with their little ones. "Hey, Jake. Throw us out a song here that the kiddos especially like. And don't say 'Baby Shark' if you value your life."

Jake roared with a deep bellow of laughter. "And here that was going to be my first suggestion. My kids are all about clapping right now. How about 'B-I-N-G-O'?"

"Hold just for a second while we get situated," called Zoey's mom, who was toting Ari while Nan carried Dante to the fire circle and sat down on a nearby log.

So much for having time to practice together before others came. It appeared they were all early today.

After a moment, Frost broke into a rousing version of "B-I-N-G-O," making sure he kept his tempo up this time and all his chords major—not that there were many chords in such a simple song. Before long they were clapping in place of the letters until there were no letters left.

"And Bingo was his name-O," Frost finished with a flourish on his guitar.

"Great job," Avery cheered. "The kids loved it."

They often sang camp songs around the fire, but usually the ones aimed at adults. Frost didn't know why he hadn't thought of singing more kids songs for the little ones.

"How about 'Five Little Ducks' next?" Zoey suggested.

It had been a while since he'd sang that song, but he'd been brushing up on his nursery rhymes so he thought he had the gist of it. He followed Zoey as she played the melody on her violin. By the time they were finished with the song, nearly everyone was gathered around the firepit, and the children had happily picked up the song; even some of the older children were singing along and encouraging the young ones.

"You have to admit this is fun," Zoey said with a suspicious gleam in her eyes.

She was up to something.

But what?

"Sure. This is fun, and the kids are apparently enjoying themselves."

"Let's do a few more."

Frost agreed, and they continued playing children's

camp and nursery songs for another half hour until everyone had arrived.

Whatever Zoey's reasons had been, Frost had really
enjoyed himself. Yet, soon he wouldn't have his babies
to sing to, and it rather felt as if Zoey was rubbing salt in
his wound, even if she didn't mean to.

He glanced at his cell phone. It was time to change
things up for his last-ditch effort to turn things around.

"Hey, Zoey," he whispered only loud enough for her
ears. "Will you play a song for me?"

"Whatever you want," she said with a smile, clearly
enjoying herself. Didn't it bother her even a little that this
was her going-away party? "A country song? A merry
Irish jig?"

"How about 'Ave Maria' by Franz Schubert?"

"Whoa. Getting a little bit heavy for a campfire, aren't
you, hon?" she quipped back, and for a moment he didn't
think she was going to play for him.

"Humor me?"

He'd beg on his knees if he had to. Actually, that was
exactly what he intended to do—but not until she started
playing. And at the moment, she didn't look as if she
would.

"I sang kiddie songs for you," he pointed out. "It only
seems fair that you play what I'd like you to play."

"Really? After everything, you want me to play classical?" Anger glinted in her eyes. He couldn't blame her. But
if she refused him, the whole rest of his surprise wasn't
going to work. He maybe should have thought of another
plan in case this one didn't work, but he hadn't. It was
this or nothing.

He laid a palm over his heart and gave her his best puppy dog look. "Please? For me?"

Daisy wagged her tail, turned in a circle, and bayed.

Zoey lifted her eyebrow at the dog. "You two are ganging up on me with those puppy dog eyes. Not fair."

"So, you'll do it?"

"Only if you'll back me up on the guitar."

"Deal."

"Even better if you sing," she suggested coyly.

He wasn't going to sing. Not this time. He wasn't even going to play guitar, but she didn't know that yet. He reached for his guitar and took a deep breath that lodged in his throat. He couldn't have sang if he'd wanted to. He did his best to smile and strummed a couple of random chords, waiting for her to start the piece.

For the longest time she stood completely still, her eyes closed, and her bow poised on the strings of her violin without playing a note. He was beginning to think she had talked herself out of it and wasn't going to play at all.

Then the first haunting notes of "Ave Maria" reverberated from her instrument. No one played the piece like Zoey, and as always, it immediately captured Frost's heart. After a few measures, the sound of a cello joined her in perfect harmony, and her eyes popped open, though she didn't miss a beat.

She must be wondering where the sound of the cello was coming from, but before she could figure it out, a viola added its unique flavor to the mix, and soon, a second violin added additional harmony to the piece.

She caught Frost's gaze and widened her eyes in question, but he just grinned. She'd figure it out soon enough, but in the meantime, she was keeping up with every note they were playing. Nothing could throw her off—not even the surprise addition of instruments.

Frost supposed he had something to prove with that—to point out that her audition *had* been a one-off and she was truly the most talented violinist he knew.

And more. But that would wait until she finished the piece.

The quartet finished "Ave Maria" to so much applause, it sounded as if there was a whole music hall full of guests instead of the handful—albeit a large handful—of Winslows seated around the bonfire.

The members of the quartet stepped out of the line of trees where they'd been playing, and hiding, and introduced themselves as members of the Colorado Symphony.

But Zoey didn't respond as Frost had thought she would. She turned pale and looked as if she was swaying on her feet. Had he goofed again?

Before the situation could get out of hand, he stepped forward and took both of Zoey's hands in his, partly to turn her to face him and partly to make sure she didn't lose her footing. She certainly appeared weak-kneed at the moment.

He cleared his throat before starting on the speech he'd been practicing for days.

"Zoey, I—did something that will probably make you mad at me." Well, that was a great start. He wanted to kick himself. "I mean—I hope not, but I understand if you are."

"You're not making sense," she pointed out. "Out with it, cowboy."

There was surprisingly little noise around the bonfire. Everyone was too curious as to what was happening between Frost and Zoey now that the music had stopped.

"Right. Well, I called the director of the Colorado Symphony."

"You did *what*?" she squawked, clearly *not* happy to hear what he'd done.

"It was only to add myself as a reference to your already amazing résumé. I know I'm not a professional musician, but I've had the advantage of having grown up next to you, so I figured I had a unique perspective on the musician and woman you are."

"I—you—go ahead," she said on a sigh. "It can't get much worse than the mess I've already made of my audition."

"That's just it," said Frost, unable to keep the cheerfulness out of his voice. "Director Lewis *didn't* cut you from the symphony after your audition. I asked her not to call so I could be the one to tell you. You're in!"

"No way." She was clearly unwilling to accept the truth.

This wasn't going well if she didn't even believe a word he was saying.

He squeezed her hands and then lifted first one and then the other to plant soft kisses along the backs. "It's true."

"But I blew that audition. How could she accept me after that?"

"I'm sure she'll want to talk to you more about it. But what I got from her was that it wasn't that you made mistakes, but that you came back from them. And the actual playing you did was magnificent. Her words."

She was still shaking her head. "So, I'm really in?"

"You are. I know you have plans in place to go to New York and you'll have to think things through, so maybe I'm making this even more complicated, but..."

He dropped to one knee before her on the cold earth.

This was either going to be the worst moment of his life or the best, but he couldn't wait any longer to find out what the rest of his life was going to look like.

Zoey watched as Frost retrieved a red velvet jewelry box out of the pocket of his fleece-lined jean jacket. Felicity quickly moved to Zoey's side and gently took her violin from her, and just in time, too, because she clapped both hands over her mouth and burst into tears. Her heart was beating so fast she was certain Frost could hear it. And probably the whole Winslow clan, too, who were sitting with eyes and ears wide open to what was happening in front of them.

And the sisters, at least, knew there was more to come after this, although there was no way for her to top Frost. Not now.

"Zoey, I have a question for you," Frost started, flipping open the lid to the red velvet box and lifting it so she could take a good look at the diamond within. She immediately knew it was the same ring he'd presented to her two years ago. That moment had been a muddle of confusion, and yet even back then her eyes had locked onto that diamond, that engagement ring that she'd known even then would be perfect for her because Frost knew her so well. Now, that knowledge brought a tug of sadness and nostalgia to the present.

He'd kept it.

But why?

Her heart was answering faster than her mind and she desperately wanted to blurt out, "Yes. Yes, yes, yes!" She wanted to make right all the wrongs of the past. But something made her wait, gave her pause. She hadn't made a final decision yet regarding where her life was going. Obviously, whether to marry Frost or not was now first and foremost, but there was so much more to it than that. Even if she didn't become engaged to Frost, it was an easy family decision to make. Staying in Colorado and playing for the symphony here would solve all their immediate problems. Frost would be able to see his children whenever he wanted to. But would he follow *his* dreams if she stayed?

This was far more complicated than just being in love with Frost because there was no doubt about that. She'd known for some time, even if she hadn't admitted it to herself.

She suddenly realized Frost was still on one knee, and he hadn't spoken his question, either, although it appeared to be obvious to everyone around. But he was gazing up at her with tear-filled eyes and didn't hasten to speak.

She reached for him and pulled him to his feet. "What is it?" she asked, because she suddenly realized *Will you marry me?* were not the words he'd been prepared to say.

"I don't want to be the one holding you back," he blurted, his words coming out on top of each other. "I don't want you making decisions because of me. I know your first choice was the Colorado Symphony, but since then you've made other plans, and you may have decided to move to New York City anyway. I want you to know I'm okay with that."

"Wait. You are?" Now she was completely confused. Was he telling her to *leave*?

"Yes." He moved the jewelry box front and center again and nodded to the string quartet, which was now a trio. They broke into a beautiful rendition of Wagner's *Lohengrin*.

The bridal chorus.

"I don't care where you go, Zoey. You can move to the moon, for all I care. To paraphrase the Book of Ruth, where you are, so also I will be. You and the babies are too important to me to let you move away. I have to be a father to Dante and Ari, and not just a man who Face-Time's them sometimes. I need to be a real part of their lives. If you need to move to New York City to fulfill your dreams, then I'm moving, too."

"Frost, you hate the big city. You'd never be happy there."

He shrugged. "In general, I would agree with you. I'm not a big city guy. But I love you. I never stopped loving you. I will be the happiest man in the world if you marry me, no matter where we end up living."

He looked as if he was going to continue, maybe to try to talk her out of it, which was typical Frost. She wasn't about to let that happen. She grabbed his scruff with both hands and pulled him in for a kiss. "Yes. Of course, yes."

She didn't even realize for a long moment that the entire audience of spectators had blown up around them, surrounding them with applause and whoops and well-wishes. Someone slipped Ari into Frost's arms and Zoey was suddenly holding Dante. They circled together, and Zoey basked in the love of her little family. Her heart was near to bursting, and she couldn't think of anything that could make the evening better.

And then she remembered.

Chapter Seventeen

Frost and Zoey cuddled close together on a log with the babies on their laps, just enjoying the amazing feeling of finally being engaged.

"I don't want to rush you, honey," Frost whispered in Zoey's ear. "But what is your heart telling you?"

"That I love you."

"The best words I have ever heard. But I meant about moving to New York."

"You'd really do that for me?"

"I would."

"Thank you. From the bottom of my heart. But there's no need. I'm staying in Colorado."

"You've already made up your mind?"

"It's best for everyone, including me. Don't worry, Frost. I *am* following my dream," she continued when he opened his mouth to protest. They knew each other so well they could anticipate each other's thoughts.

He let out a breath and Zoey smiled tenderly. He really would have followed her and the twins to New York City, but he was happy he didn't need to.

He leaned in again and Zoey closed her eyes, expecting sweet nothings from Frost's rumbling voice. Instead, he had a question. "Why are all my sisters staring at us?" he asked.

Zoey's eyes popped open, and she looked around. Sure enough, the Winslow ladies were all watching them like hawks, and it wasn't because they thought it was cute that she and Frost had just become engaged.

"Yeah. There's one more thing I forgot to mention."

"Mmm. And what is that?" He smiled at her, his silver-blue eyes gleaming in the firelight.

"Well, you know how you kind of did something behind my back and you weren't sure how I would take it? I…um…did something similar." The last words came out in a rush.

"You what?"

"Please don't kill me. We just now got engaged. I'd like to at least live until our wedding day."

"Okay. I may possibly hang you upside down by your toes, but I promise not to kill you. Now tell me. What did you do?"

She reached for the diaper bag and pulled out a folder. Avery and Jake immediately stepped forward to take the twins from them.

Frost's eyes widened as his sister and her husband absconded with the children. "This just gets curiouser and curiouser," he said, mimicking *Alice in Wonderland.* "You aren't going to pop a white rabbit out of that file folder, are you?"

"No, but that's quite apropos, now that I think about it. You're late for a very important date."

"Yeah? Please tell me you have a calendar inside to pick our wedding date. The sooner, the better, although I know you want the works with your wedding, so I'll try to be patient."

She playfully clapped his shoulder. "No, it's not a wedding calendar, you big goof. We'll get to that soon. Not tonight, though. I didn't even know you were going to propose to me."

"True." He flashed her a half smile she'd often told him she'd found attractive. He wanted to use every tool in his tool chest on this of all evenings. "So?"

She audibly exhaled and slid the folder onto his lap. He wrapped his arm around her and pulled her close to him, spooning her back with his chest.

"What's this then?" he asked as he pulled out a letter with the University of Northern Colorado-Greeley banner.

"Read it," she whispered.

"Dear Mr. Winslow," he read aloud. "We are happy to offer you a spot in next year's freshman class. Information on your music auditions will be forthcoming by separate cover."

Emotions crowded one over the other in a rush.

Joy. Confusion. Amazement. Fear.

He set down the paper and turned so he could meet her gaze.

"What is this?"

"I should think that would be obvious," Zoey answered a little shakily. She couldn't tell by his expression how he felt about what he'd just read.

"I know what it is. I guess the better question is how did it happen? Once I found out about the twins, I didn't send in an application."

"No, but I did. I saw it on your desk the night we got snowed in at your house and I... I took it. I felt like if you wouldn't send it in and find out where God might be leading you, I would. This at least gives you options." It had sounded better as a thought than it did now coming out of her mouth.

"I have to be able to provide for Dante and Ari, and that means working full time."

"You're thinking too linearly. And you're not considering the full picture." Was this going to be their first big fight as an engaged couple? And in front of their families. How humiliating.

"Enlighten me," he whispered, his blond eyebrows lowering under the brim of his hat.

"First, it's only a few years, and when you're finished, you'll have a teaching degree and a regular job that you love."

"I like my job."

"Yes, but it's not your dream job."

She decided to push ahead. "You can still work weekends at the farm, both while you're in school and when you're teaching at the elementary school."

He didn't argue that point, but thoughtfully stroked his jaw instead.

Stubborn Winslow.

"Another thing I'd like to point out is that I'll also be working during this time. The care and feeding of the twins isn't all on you, you know. We'll be a two-income household and even with you going to school, we should do just fine."

"Humph."

She waited a moment, but he didn't elaborate.

"Is that a good humph or a bad humph?" she finally asked.

He curled a hand around her neck and pulled her to him, answering her with a kiss.

"Good, because I went to the effort of looking around Greeley for apartments, something that will fit a family of four. I've got several flyers inside that folder you set aside."

"Is there anything you haven't thought of?" he asked, grinning and shaking his head. "It seems to me you have everything in your capable hands."

"Everything except my violin," she said, standing and reaching out to him. "I'd like to do a little fiddling now, and maybe even play a classical piece or two since we have a string quartet here."

"Play to your heart's content, my love. I've paid the quartet for the whole evening."

"You've paid for a lifetime. Now come and join me."

Hearts, instruments and voices. Just as the Lord had always intended it to be.

* * * * *

Dear Reader,

Thank you for reading Frost's story, the sixth and final Winslow sibling. He's been around since the very first book in the Rocky Mountain Family series, so I felt as if I already knew him well when I started revealing his gentle heart. As someone in whose life music plays a huge part (pun intended!), I especially love that Frost is a man of music, and that this connection strengthens his relationship with Zoey. I will miss the Winslow family bonfires, where all the characters from previous stories unite to celebrate.

I hope you enjoyed reading the Rocky Mountain Family series as much as I loved writing it.

I'm always delighted to hear from you, and I love to connect socially. To get regular updates, please visit my website and sign up for my newsletter at https://www.debkastnerbooks.com. Come join me on Facebook at *DebKastnerBooks*, or catch me on Twitter or Instagram @debkastner.

Please know that I pray for each and every one of you without ceasing. When I sit down to write it is with you in mind.

Dare to Dream,
Deb Kastner